THE SARATOGA DECEPTION
A Mystery Novel of the American Revolution

STEVE LEADLEY

This book is a work of historical fiction.
Names, characters, places, and incidents
are either products of the author's imagination
or are used in a historical context to further the story's plot.

A Beach Reeds publication

Cover Art: *The Death of Jane McCrea* by John Vanderlyn c. 1804

Look for other books by Steve Leadley at:

www.steveleadleyauthorpage.weebly.com

ISBN: 978-0-9800944-5-9

Library of Congress Cataloging-in-Publication Data
Leadley, Steve
Saratoga Deception, The/ Steve Leadley
Beach Reeds, 2013

Historical Fiction/American Revolution/Revolutionary War/ /Historical
Mystery

Chapter 1

"Jane, I implore you to come with me," the tall man in the colonel's uniform pleaded as he shoved various items into his saddle bag. "General Burgoyne's army is on the way..."

"John," she interrupted, "that is precisely *why* I won't leave! I have just received a letter from David. He is sending for me. By nightfall I will be safely in the British camp, and he and I will be reunited."

The Patriot adjusted his sword as he crossed the room. He exhaled heavily before looking his younger sister squarely in the eyes. "Janey, Burgoyne's advance scouts will be Indians. David, even General Burgoyne, would certainly be honorable enough to overlook the fact that you have been living in my home and grant you safe passage-- but the Indians are savage. If they learn that you chose to reside under the roof of an officer of the American forces, they could use it as an excuse to..." he bit his lip, unable to finish the sentence.

The girl pushed back her long blonde locks and took hold of her older brother's hands. "John, I must go. You know that I must." There followed an unsettling silence before she brushed her hands over the lapels of his coat in a motherly fashion, dusting away a speck or two of lint. "Now, it is *you* who must go. Hurry or you will miss the rendezvous with your regiment. I will communicate with you when I can." After a few somber words of farewell, the colonel slipped from the house and galloped off.

1

The dust from her brother's departure still hung in the air as Jane stepped off of the porch. She shouldered her bag and walked off northward. Within a half an hour she arrived at the home of the widow Sara McNeil, herself a Loyalist and cousin of British general Simon Fraser, Burgoyne's subordinate.

The elderly woman hastened her inside the log cabin. "Oh my dear, I am glad that you are here. Did you hear the musket-fire when you were on the road?"

"Musket-fire? No, no I didn't."

"Oh... Well I suppose that it came from the north." The old woman glanced around nervously. "David did instruct you to meet me here, then?" she asked uneasily. "I have not had any word myself from any of our friends... I pray that you will see to it that I am taken with you to the general's camp?"

Jane smiled reassuringly. "Yes, of course," she soothed. "David is sending a band of scouts..."

"Scouts?" the white haired woman squawked. "Savages?" the fear in her voice caused its pitch to raise into a falsetto tone.

Jane pushed her beautiful blond hair from her eyes, and patted the old woman's hand reassuringly. "They are in advance of the army. You do want to reach General Burgoyne's headquarters as quickly as possible, don't you?"

The sound of the recent musket barrage echoed in Mrs. McNeil's mind. "Yes, I believe that would be best. And if David trusts them, I suppose that should be good enough for me," she laughed disingenuously, trying to mask her trepidation.

A moment after the uneasy cackle left Sara McNeil's lips, the door burst open. There, framed in the doorway was the dark form of an Indian warrior. The sinewy shape was devoid of clothing from the waist upward and strange patterns of red and black paint danced across his muscular shoulders and chest. In the crook of his arm rested a rifle. A tomahawk dangled from one hip while the handle of a large knife protruded from a buckskin sheath upon the other. As he stepped further into the

2

room, the shadows retreated from his face, exposing fierce features and the peculiar Mohawk hairstyle worn by natives of the region. His neck and face were covered in black war-paint, a distinctive white streak of paint resembling lightning slashed diagonally across his face. Several more braves filed in behind this terrifying warrior.

Sara McNeil's hand shook fearfully as she furtively reached behind her, feeling hopelessly for the fireplace poker that leaned against the hearth. Jane however stepped boldly forward.

"I am Jane McCrea and this is Mrs. McNeil. Did Lieutenant Jones send you to collect us?"

At first, the warrior appeared not to hear her, his eyes seemingly fixated upon the striking golden tresses that fell gently upon the girl's shoulders. Suddenly his eyes moved to hers and his chin dropped in a slight nod. He struck his chest with his palm and bluntly introduced himself, "Le Loup. Come," he said, extending his arm and making the corresponding hand signal to the women.

"You see," Jane said, turning a smile upon her frightened companion. "They were sent by David."

Sara seemed a bit more relaxed as the women left the abode and the scouts helped them each upon a horse. The Indians were afoot, and the mounts' civilian saddles hinted that the animals were likely captured booty in some recent raid as opposed to being supplied by the Indians' British patrons.

The scouts took hold of the bridles and began to lead the horses in the direction of Burgoyne's invading army. The Indians had not uttered a single word upon the trail and an eerie silence hung over the desolate path that cut through the dense forest of pine and oak. They were not more than a quarter mile from Mrs. McNeil's home, when at a fork the party ran into another band of Indians. Le Loup signaled his men to a halt and advanced the fifty feet or so to confer with the leader of the new arrivals. Sara began to nervously finger the horn of her saddle.

3

The two Indians began to raise their voices, and although the language was guttural gibberish to the two ladies, it was obvious that the conversation had become heated. Jane curiously scrutinized the pair. She knew the Indians to be a generally stoic breed and her interest grew as emphatic gesticulations began to accompany the fiery argument.

"What... What do you suppose is going on?" Sara stammered fretfully.

"I'm not sure..." Jane returned, without taking her eyes from the spectacle.

Hastily Le Loup returned, however his recent antagonist was at his heels. Le Loup uttered a few unintelligible words to his men, which had the effect of the warrior holding the reins of Sara's pony handing them over to the leader of the second faction. As the Indian began to lead Mrs. McNeil away, the older woman spun frantically in her saddle.

"Jane! Jane! What is going on? Why are they separating us?"

"Great Father... Burgoyne..." the brave leading Sara's mount stated, struggling mightily with the pronunciation of the general's name. He placed his hand upon his heart and then pointed forward.

"It's alright!" Jane called ahead reassuringly. "I think that group is taking you to the general's camp where this band is supposed to escort me to David! He said in his letter that he may be left to garrison Ticonderoga and might not be presently with General Burgoyne!"

"Alright, Jane! Have David bring you to visit me!" she yelled back as she was led further down the path. If Sara was not truly mollified by Jane's explanation, she at least made an effective show of it. Le Loup uttered a throaty order and his group headed off, leading Jane's horse down the other branch in the road.

4

They had been travelling for about twenty minutes when Le Loup abruptly threw up a hand, signaling a sudden halt. The warrior leading Jane's pony stopped, handing the reins to Le Loup. He hurried ahead, stopping a hundred yards or so in advance. Another raced back down the trail an equal distance and appeared to be scanning the roadway from which they came. "What is it?" Jane asked Le Loup. "What is it?" she asked again, keeping her voice low, suspecting that the scouts detected something unperceivable to the senses of a white woman.

Suddenly, the Indian grabbed the girl by the collar and yanked her from the saddle. She crashed to the ground, more astonished than dazed. Jane brushed the yellow locks from her eyes just in time to see a glint from the tomahawk before it buried itself in her skull.

VAN HORNE HOUSE
MIDDLEBROOK, NEW JERSEY
HEADQUARTERS OF
GENERAL WILLIAM ALEXANDER
(WASHINGTON'S SECOND IN COMMAND)

The door had been left slightly ajar and the young man leaned forward from the hard wooden chair upon which he sat, straining to hear through the thin crack. His imagination had embellished the hard, factual report the colonel in the next room had read to General Alexander[1], and he inched forward expectantly, his curiosity overwhelming his sense of soldierly decorum.

---

[1] The American General William Alexander was more commonly known as "Lord Stirling" as he professed to be heir to a Scottish title. In order to avoid confusing the man with one on the crown's side in the war, he is referred to as Alexander throughout this story.

"Is that an accurate account?" The general's unmistakable voice drifted to the anteroom.

"It is the one we've received from our people," the colonel returned. "However Burgoyne's report states that the girl was shot by militiamen who had attacked the Indians as they tried to bring her safely through his lines."

The general's tread could be heard pacing the boards before he asked, "But the Indians did return to Burgoyne's encampment with her scalp?"

"Yes, sir," the colonel replied. "But Burgoyne's communiqué states that they only took their trophy after she had been killed by Continentals."

There was a long pause as the pacing of the general began again. Abruptly the commander stopped and the scraping of a chair indicated that he had taken a seat. "Sit down, Colonel," he said, his voice betraying a tone that he may be about to bring news not fully welcome to his subordinate's ears. "We need to call in -----." The name had been rendered inaudible as a wagon rumbled past the window.

"Sir..." the aggravation was evident in the colonel's voice. "Do you really think that is wise?"

There was another long pause as if the general was weighing the other man's words. "Burgoyne's plan is to link up with the armies of St. Leger and Howe. St. Leger is to come east down the Mohawk River and General Howe is supposed to proceed north out of New York City. If successful they would cut New England off from the rest of the country..." Alexander's voice trailed off as if he were contemplating the mortal blow Burgoyne's plan could deal their cause if it were to come to fruition.

"General Gates is going to have his hands full," Alexander continued. "However, if it is true that the McCrea woman was actually murdered by Burgoyne's scouts, the locals would be outraged. If it got out that the British could not control their

6

Indians, hundreds, perhaps even thousands of men would rush to join General Gates' forces desperate to drive the enemy from the region."

"General Gates?" the colonel blurted, evidently surprised.

"Yes, Congress is blaming General Schuyler for the loss of Ticonderoga. They are going to replace him with Horatio Gates."

"Sir…" the colonel appeared to be choosing his words cautiously, to best affect his desired result. "…I am sure that General Gates can handle the situation. There is no need to involve *him*," he said, referring to the man whose name had been obscured by the passing of the wagon. "If we let our people's version of the story spread we will gain the same outcome without the potential hazards *he* brings to the situation."

A gentle tapping sounded as the general drummed his fingers upon his desk while formulating his reply. "No Colonel, that simply won't do. If our explanation does not accurately reflect the events, and we are found out to be liars, too much would be lost. Our revolution is one of ideals. Those ideals are what bring men to fight for the cause. If it is learned that we have manipulated the truth for our own purposes we would likely lose double; perhaps triple the number of men we might temporarily gain with such a ruse. We must never compromise our principles if we are to prevail."

"Jeffrey," the general continued, trying to placate the colonel by addressing him by his first name. "I know that you don't like him," he referred again to the mysterious man, "but didn't he prove himself with that business up in Boston? And what about his success with the Hessians? And that issue in Manhattan?"

The colonel grunted, interrupting his superior. "What if he should decide to disregard orders? You know that he will do exactly as he pleases. He does not respect authority!" his voice rose in anger.

7

General Alexander was silent again for a maddening duration. "Your concerns are valid, of course. But, there is no point arguing about it further. This comes directly from the commander-in-chief."

"It does?" the colonel sounded shocked. "Why would Washington involve himself in something so trivial?"

"Trivial? The death of one country girl may not seem monumental, but I've already explained what is at stake should the British accomplish their goal in isolating New England. Remember, Burgoyne has already retaken the fort at Ticonderoga. You must concede that we cannot overlook any means that might help us add strength to General Gates' army."

"Yes..." the colonel mused, "but it seems as if there must be something more for General Washington to show such interest..."

The chair grated on the floor as General Alexander stood. There was a hint of jest in his voice as he needled, "You are the one so concerned about respecting authority Colonel, so rather than question our commanding general's intentions I suggest you follow his orders without further complaint."

As the footsteps neared the door the young soldier quickly pulled himself back from the edge of his seat, hoping that the two men would not suspect that he had been eavesdropping. As they stepped through the doorway, the young man jumped to attention, holding his salute.

General Alexander returned the gesture and placed an affectionate hand upon the young officer's shoulder. "Captain Shelby, it is good to see you. I hope that you are well?"

"Yes, sir. Thank you sir."

8

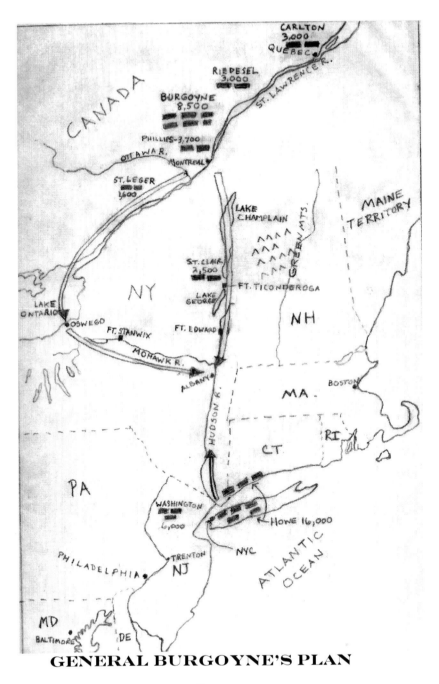

GENERAL BURGOYNE'S PLAN

"When you next write Madeline give my best, Jeffrey," Alexander said turning back to Colonel Williams.

The colonel tucked a packet of folded papers into his breast pocket. "I shall, sir." He saluted his superior and turned to the young soldier, his voice assuming a more surly tone as he grumbled, "Come with me, Captain."

Colonel Williams led the way out to the encampment. His tread was more the stomp of a petulant child than the gait of a regal officer and the captain could hear him muttering to himself as he plodded along. Finally they reached the colonel's tent where he ducked under the flap. He had not beckoned the captain to follow, so the confused soldier waited outside.

"Captain Shelby! Where are you? Confound it!" The colonel's churlish bellow indicated that he was supposed to have trailed his superior, a mistake the captain hastened to rectify by dashing through the portal.

"Here, sir. I'm sorry, I wasn't sure if you wanted me to follow..." he apologized.

The colonel poured himself a glass of amber liquid and fell back into a rickety camp chair. As he drained the glass, he motioned for Shelby to take a seat upon the stool beside the small table that acted as a makeshift desk. Colonel Williams pulled the packet of papers from his coat and read them over, shaking his head and exhaling heavily.

"Captain, how old are you? Nineteen perhaps?" Williams asked, rubbing tired eyes with the forefinger and thumb of his left hand.

"Twenty sir."

"This war has already made an old man of me," he said, massaging the bridge of his nose. He sighed heavily before continuing. "You are to leave here tomorrow morning and head to Ringwood. There you are to go to the Twin Oaks Tavern and deliver this packet to a Mister..." he scanned the document before continuing, "...Fox. He is using his true name; I suppose

10

it is an appropriate moniker," he chuckled under his breath as he refilled his glass.

An uneasy silence followed as the colonel stared into his tumbler, swirling its contents. "Sir, am I to wait for a reply?" Captain Shelby asked, breaking the stillness.

The colonel smiled without halting his peculiar ritual. "That is an interesting question," he coyly replied before gulping down the drink. "If he sends you back, by all means report to me."

A puzzled look clouded over Shelby's face. "Sir, *if* he sends me back? I don't quite under—"

"Pour me another will you, Captain?" the colonel interrupted as he lit a candle and heated a stamp of wax over the flame. As Shelby complied, Colonel Williams refolded the papers and sealed them closed with the hot wax. "Here, Shelby," he handed the packet to the captain. His words were a bit slurred, the liquor having apparently gained some influence. "Now leave me, I have other work to do."

"But sir," he said as he stood, about to inquire again about the "if," however the aggravated expression upon the colonel's face made him think better of it. "Sir, how will I know this Mr. Fox?"

Colonel Williams laughed heartily. "Oh, you'll know him, my boy... Unless of course he doesn't want you to," it was unclear if this statement was purposefully cryptic or the result of inebriation. "No matter though, he'll know you. Now be on your way already," he quipped, returning the captain's salute with a halfhearted one of his own.

11

Chapter 2

The heat was staggering. Even though he longed to reach his destination and be free of the dusty road he dared not push his horse too hard. By early afternoon the sky had clouded over but this had done little to remedy the situation as the blazing warmth of the sun had merely segued into an oppressive, oven-like swelter.

The monotonous tread of his mount and exhaustive temperature caused the captain's thoughts to roam and when a roll of thunder sounded off to the west, the lonely messenger snapped upright in the saddle momentarily mistaking the noise for canon-fire. It had been only a month before that he had been with General Alexander when they had engaged Howe at Scotch Pines and it had been the British canon that had compelled them into a strategic retreat. He smiled to himself at the irony that the heat he so despised at the moment had been of such service that day, forcing Howe to end his pursuit.

As the reminiscence of the battle faded, his fatigued mind engaged itself in debate as to whether the cooling effects of a downpour would be worth the damage it would do to his appearance and more seriously, the danger it might bring in the form of lightning. At last he concluded that these contemplations were irrelevant since fate alone could decide such issues.

Fortune had chosen to spare Shelby both relief and danger as the rumbling drifted northward rather than rendezvous with the weary traveler. It was early evening when his horse ambled into the sleepy hamlet of Ringwood. The surrounding Ramapo

Mountains had begun to cast long shadows and he had to squint to read the placards that adorned the town's structures.

A ramshackle cart hauling wood was about to pass in the opposite direction when leaning from his saddle, Shelby grabbed the gray nag's reins close to the bridle bringing the wagon to a halt. "Pardon," he said to the grizzled old driver. "Can you please direct me to the Twin Oaks?"

The codger pushed back his floppy hat and scanned the captain's uniform through narrowed eyes. He leaned over toward the ground to discharge a spittle of tobacco, but suddenly he thought better of doing this so near the soldier and bent toward the opposite side of his cart before performing the action. Finally, he said, "Over yonder," jerking a thumb toward a building on the other side of the street.

"Thank you," Shelby returned, tipping his tricorne hat after releasing the man's horse.

Even as daylight retreated over the horizon, the captain could make out the tavern's rustic, unpainted clapboard siding. The inn was not in disrepair, but it was evident that its clientele were not of a cosmopolitan rank. An oval sign hung from an exposed beam that protruded from the porch roof. The board was devoid of wording, instead a rudimentary hand-painted rendition of a pair of oak trees gently swayed in the merciful breeze that had just stirred.

Shelby dismounted and tightened the reins around the hitching post. He unstrapped his saddle bags and tossed them over his shoulder, then adjusted the strap that held his sword. The captain patted the chestnut head of his mount as he peered through a dusty window. The placid reflection of lamplight was all that he could observe, but the gentle murmur that met his ears indicated that perhaps as many as a dozen patrons were in attendance. He straightened his coat, stiffened his back and pushed in through the door.

13

Inside most of the dozen tables were occupied by a menagerie of men and women. Off to his left, a pair of men leaned against the far end of the bar. At the moment, Shelby was most concerned about his horse and ducked the tray of a serving girl as she whisked past. He strode over to the bar to engage the large man who stood behind it polishing a glass. Spying the officer, the barkeeper immediately hastened over. "You look as if you've been on the road awhile, sir, can I get you a tankard?" he asked with the gratuitous nature of one whose income depends upon service.

"Absolutely," Shelby returned, removing his hat and placing it upon the counter. "And I need someone to attend to my horse. He requires water and a spell without his saddle would do him no harm either."

The bartender smiled, revealing a vacancy of two teeth. "No trouble there, sir," he replied, as he tossed a mug in front of Shelby and repeated the captain's request to a boy who had emerged from a back room. Before the captain could comment further, one of the men at the end of the bar summoned the innkeeper and he shuffled off to his duty. He watched the barman refill the drink of the man, but was also aware of the hushed comments the customer made to his companion as they suspiciously scrutinized him.

Despite being warm, the ale was most welcome to Shelby's parched throat. He gratefully downed a third of the glass's contents before resting it on the counter. After a sigh of contentment, he turned his attention to the room's occupants. "I'd know him?" he mumbled to himself quizzically, recalling Colonel Williams' strange statement. He began his survey with the pair at the end of the bar before moving his gaze from table to table. None of those he surveyed appeared distinct in the slightest. All of the patrons, both male and female, looked to be nothing more than common townsfolk or their ruddy farming neighbors. He had already decided that asking the barman if he

14

knew a "Mr. Fox" would be a last resort, not wanting to reveal his quest to another unless it were absolutely necessary. But after his tiring ride he was ready to compromise such a precaution. As he turned to summon the man, he caught sight of a leg poking out from a nook behind the stonework of the fireplace.

Although the sudden realization of a hidden occupant would certainly have been enough to draw the weary seeker's attention, the uniqueness of this particular appendage doubled his interest. The other people in the room were all adorned with the traditional footwear one would expect to find in such a place; the black leather boots and buckled shoes of the men and women were notably indistinct. However, the right leg that protruded from behind the hearth wore a dark buckskin moccasin laced up to the knee. Odder still, one would expect the rest of such a leg to be housed in the material of a woodsman or perhaps the bare tawny skin of an Indian. Yet, instead rose the black knickered breeches associated with a more civilized society.

The captain took another swig from his mug as he curiously leaned to one side, trying to bring more of the individual into view. However, the stonework of the hearth still obscured further observation. He placed his hat upon his head and swallowed the remainder in his mug. Tossing his saddlebags over his shoulder he then sauntered away from the bar. Slowly he began to walk across the room. As he rounded the corner of the fireplace he was surprised by the visage of the complete figure. There, seated alone, sat a spectacled man seemingly deeply engrossed in a leather-bound volume. The upper half of this individual was attired in a fine linen shirt. A plain, though quality black frockcoat lay neatly folded over another chair at his table. Atop this unique fellow's head sat the broad-brimmed hat of a Quaker, being the same raven hue as his coat and pants. The man reclined leisurely in his chair, rhythmically rocking back on its hind legs. His frontier style moccasins were certainly out of

15

place with his Quaker dress, but so were two items which sat upon the table: a powder horn and a cartridge box.

Without looking up from his book the man casually said, "Have a seat, Captain."

The words somewhat startled the young soldier as he imagined that the peculiarly dressed man at the table had been unaware of his presence. He hurriedly draped his saddle bags over one of the chairs and ducked under the baldrick that held his sword. After removing the weapon, he hung it over the same chair as his bags.

"Mr. Fox?" he asked quietly as he took a seat.

The oddly clad individual across the table had yet to look up from his book and the awkward silence that followed caused Shelby some misgivings. "I am sorry," he said finally, beginning to stand, "I must have the wrong..."

"No, you have the right man," he interrupted but said nothing further. Shelby fell back into his seat and suffered through the silence once again. From this vantage point, he could read the Greek letters embossed on the book's cover. "*The Iliad?*" he translated in his head. "An odd book for a Quaker to be reading," he thought to himself, juxtaposing the epic tale of warfare with the pacifist sect. Two full minutes passed as the man continued reading. Growing somewhat perturbed, he blurted, "Mr. Fox, I have been sent..."

"Forgive me," Fox cut him off, draping the ribbon that hung from the binding to mark the page before closing the book. "I was just at the end of the chapter," he stated, removing his glasses. As he folded his spectacles and neatly tucked them into a case upon the table, the captain studied the man further, more than a little annoyed that he had selfishly put his own rather insignificant indulgence ahead of Shelby's mission. Fox appeared to be in his early to mid-thirties. The hair that peaked from beneath his hat was sandy in color and his eyes were a grayish-blue. Although eyeglasses usually affix a scholarly air

16

to the wearer, they had seemed out of place on this man. He was powerfully built and an inch or two over six feet in height. His face was tanner than one tending to bookish activities and Shelby's impression was that the Quaker clothing was more out of place upon him than the woodsman's moccasins.

"Yes, well I have been sent to deliver this to you," Shelby said with a hint of exasperation as he removed the packet from his breast pocket and dropped it in the center of the table.

Fox placed his hand atop the papers and slid them closer. He reached for his eyeglass case but apparently thought better of it. Abruptly, he let go of the packet and looked up at Shelby. A crooked smile formed on the left side of his mouth. "Captain, I think I would prefer it if *you* told me what this was about."

Shelby had been staring at the papers as Fox dragged them across the table but this request startled the young soldier and his eyes suddenly darted upward to meet those of the other man.

"I am sorry, Mr. Fox," he said, his face flushing, "but I am merely a messenger sent to deliver that packet to you."

The curious smile remained as Fox gave a little silent laugh as if he had told himself a joke. "Yes... Well be that as it may Captain, I would still rather hear the particulars from you."

Shelby opened his mouth to reply, but Fox continued, "Prior to protesting further, I warn you not to perjure yourself before the Lord. From what I understand, your Pope directs you to uphold the Commandments--even the one against lying." He chuckled silently to himself again.

The young man's mind inadvertently cycled through a series of confused thoughts. "How does he know that I am aware of the contents of the message? How could he possibly know that I am Catholic?" Mystification and resentment washed over him but these sentiments quickly faded as he succumbed to the realization that any charade would be futile.

A smile spread across the young man's face as he acquiesced and he quietly commenced reiterating the particulars of the

17

report he had overheard outside of the general's office. Although forthcoming about the conflicting details of Miss McCrea's death, and the dire consequences they might pose to the future of the revolution, he made no mention of Colonel Williams' opposition to his involvement.

A sudden sense of alarm occurred to Shelby as he concluded. "Mr. Fox, I assure you that I had not intended to eavesdrop. The door was left open to some degree and I had not the authority to shut it or to wait outside. The colonel had told me to take a seat, and..."

Fox arrested his ramblings with an indifferent wave of his hand and an accompanying sideways smirk. "You need not rationalize it to me, lad-- and you should stop trying to do so to yourself as well." He pulled his reading glasses from their case and broke the wax seal on the packet. "Let's see if there is anything in these papers you haven't already related."

"Oh my!" Fox broke off reading. Shelby was startled, thinking he had come across something dreadful in the pages. However, the truth was far less dramatic but much more welcome. "You must be famished, Captain! How inconsiderate of me." He called the serving girl over and asked her to bring the soldier a plate. "I'm afraid there is no menu, so to speak. It is pork tonight. Is that alright, Captain?"

Shelby smiled. "Yes, that would be excellent. I had a biscuit on the road this morning, but have not eaten since. Thank you."

Fox returned to the letter but addressed his companion as he read. "The pork is not bad, although I doubt that you will find it as appetizing as the crabs or rockfish you Marylanders pull from the Chesapeake."

Shelby shot a perplexed look at the man across the table, puzzling over this latest feat of clairvoyance. However, Mr. Fox's countenance did not fluctuate in the least as he continued to scan the documents in hand.

Fox was still paging through the papers while the captain gratefully dug into his steaming dinner. "Bring the gentleman another stout my dear, would you please, and I would be much obliged if you would refill my tea," he said, pushing his cup in her direction.

Between mouthfuls Shelby said quietly, "General Alexander told the colonel that it was General Washington who wanted you brought into this matter." He studied Fox's face as he made this revelation, curious to see what reaction it would bring or what his reply might disclose. However the man merely acknowledged with a grunt as he finished reading and then refolded the packet. He dipped the end of the papers through the top of the lamp which sat upon the table and turned them over until the message was consumed in flames. He then quickly leaned forward and tossed the burning item into the fireplace.

After the girl had deposited their respective beverages and retreated once more, Shelby looked up from his plate, about to ask Fox if he had any message he wanted transmitted back to Colonel Williams. However he found his eccentric tablemate to be once again engrossed in his book. The captain shrugged his shoulders, content to forego further conversation so that he might hungrily devour the remnants of his dinner. After he finished eating he sat in quiet awkwardness hoping that Mr. Fox would soon conclude his latest chapter. Finally, he reached for the ribbon. As he pushed the marker in place with his right hand, he removed his hat with his left and fanned his face as if the grueling heat of the day had just now reached him.

"So, Mr. Fox do you have any message you would like me to convey to..." he never completed the sentence as he was rocked by a hard shove from behind.

"Where's your regiment, soldier boy? You're a brave one, venturing so far from camp alone."

Shelby turned to find the two men from the bar looming over him. In one motion the captain was on his feet, his thin, five foot

19

ten inch frame rising half a head over the two more stoutly built antagonists. Before he could utter a rebuke, Mr. Fox calmly interjected, "Now brothers, there's no need for hostility," as he nonchalantly took a sip of his tea.

"Oh, but we think there is," the second one laughed.

"Go about your business," Shelby coldly said.

"What happens in this tavern *is* our business, soldier boy," the first man barked back. "And we think it's time you were leaving." He slapped a grubby paw upon the captain's shoulder and reached his other hand toward Shelby's lapel as if he planned on physically tossing him from the establishment. His second hand never made contact however, as the captain drove a vicious short left into his antagonist's nose. The man fell backward, landing his buttocks upon the floor. It was but a fraction of a second before the man's friend jumped into the fray. He grabbed a two foot log from the wood bin next to the fireplace and swung it at the officer's head. Shelby ducked the blow and in the same motion grabbed the hilt of his sword hanging from the chair next to him and drew the blade from its scabbard. Rather than swing with the cutting edge, he smashed the man's jaw with the weapon's hand-guard. The second opponent crumpled backward, joining his friend upon the floor. Both men sat upon the wide, dusty planking, one with his hands clasped over his bleeding nose, the other shaking the cobwebs from his brain as he rubbed his bruised jaw.

The altercation had lasted all of five seconds. Patrons lucky enough to have caught sight of this entertainment began jovially recapping the battle for those who had disappointingly missed it. Captain Shelby stood stoically over the two men saber in hand, awaiting their next move. Grumbling, the pair picked themselves up and skulked out of the tavern. Several customers patted them on their backs and joked consoling words as they departed.

20

Shelby re-sheathed his blade and returned to his seat where he surprisingly found Mr. Fox still casually sipping his tea. "It is blokes like that that give country-folk a bad name," he quipped with his accompanying muted laugh. The captain returned the smile, more out of bemused curiosity at the man's eccentric nature than from any sense of mirth.

The bartender hustled over stating, "I'm sorry about that sir, they ain't bad lads, and they ain't Tories neither. I suspect they just had a bit too much of the lager and thought they'd have a lark."

"It is too late for me to return tonight, do you have lodgings available?" he asked, ignoring the man's apology.

"No sir, the only room we have is occupied by your friend here--"

"Hardly a problem," Fox broke in. "Have someone bring his things up."

The innkeeper nodded and shuffled off.

"Thank you, Mr. Fox. I will try to be of little inconvenience. I plan to head back to camp as early as possible."

Fox chuckled quietly. "I hope it is you who are not inconvenienced, Captain. You won't be returning to camp. The documents you brought confirmed that I could retain you if I thought you would be of any value in this matter. I have decided that you could in fact be of some use."

Chapter 3

The pair left the inn just after daybreak and headed northward into the wilds of New York. The previous night Shelby would have liked to have queried Mr. Fox further, about a good many things, but the man insisted that they retire early so that they would be well rested when they got underway upon the morrow. The plan had worked well for Mr. Fox, who seemed to drift off the moment he reclined upon the bed. However, the young captain had found sleeping difficult. Colonel Williams' queer statement *if he sends you back* suddenly made perfect sense. His mind sifted through the events surrounding the death of Miss McCrea and the consequences the woman's demise might hold for the fledgling country. However as he floated into unconsciousness Shelby had found himself wondering about the man sharing his room and what might have induced General Washington to involve this extremely peculiar individual in this matter.

Fox's mottled gray horse led the way down the narrow trail. With a mixture of admiration and confusion Shelby scrutinized the Pennsylvania long rifle slung across the back of the man in front of him. "That looks to be a fine rifle," he finally said, breaking the somber silence that had hung over the pair since the trek began.

Rather than reply to the captain's comment, without looking back he returned, "Are you armed beyond that saber of yours?"

"I have a brace of dragoon pistols in my bags."

"About a mile farther is a stream. When we stop to water the horses you had better load them and tuck them into your belt."

"Do you expect trouble?"

Although Shelby could not see his face, he was certain that it wore that characteristic sideways grin as he replied, "No, but I would rather not be taken unawares should the unexpected decide to show itself."

The captain stared again at the rifle. "You're a Quaker, aren't you?"

There was a long pause before Fox returned, "Why do you ask?"

"It's just that you appear to be, yet the Quakers are pacifists. I suspected it was such beliefs that caused you to sit idly by when those two accosted me in the tavern," he said with just a hint of resentment. "Is the rifle just for show then, in hopes of scaring off any ruffians or Indians?"

Several moments passed before Fox said over his shoulder, "No, the rifle is not a contrivance. And I could not intervene at the inn or I would have wasted my money."

Shelby laughed. "I hardly think your tea would have gone cold in the duration it took to dispatch that lot."

"I must agree with you there, Captain. No, I meant the dollar I paid those two to confront you."

A stunned silence fell over the rider. Suddenly he spurred his horse and came alongside Mr. Fox as the trail had just widened out. "Pardon? You paid them to waylay me?" he asked incredulously.

Fox smiled at him mischievously. "I am sorry about that, but I had to know if you could handle yourself. I was aware that they were sending a junior officer to me, and that I might be entitled to keep him on. However, I had no idea who they were sending or what kind of fighting abilities he might possess. Before you arrived I had arranged for those boys to come over and confront you if I were to signal by fanning myself with my hat."

The captain's shocked face spread into a smile of his own. "I am glad that I passed your test, Mr. Fox as the consequences for having failed it would have been painful in the most literal sense. However, you could have just asked me. I have been with Washington's army since Long Island and have seen action in practically every battle since."

"It is not your prowess upon the field that concerned me," he replied. "There is no doubt that such engagements can strengthen one's fortitude and indicate a soldier's bravery. But when confronting another army, soldiers are supported by hundreds of their comrades, and most of the fighting is done at arm's length. It is a different kind of martial skills that are needed in close-quarter combat. I assure you Captain that the neutral ground between the two armies is perhaps more dangerous than the battlefield. There are roving bands of criminals who murder in the name of this side or that, but are merely out to thieve from the innocent. Not to mention the war parties; but of course you are already aware of the Indians' barbarism."

A sudden thought dawned on the young officer. "I had assumed that your contact had given you information about me, yet you say that you did not know who the messenger would be. How then did you know so much about me?"

"I know almost nothing about you, Captain."

"You knew that I am from Maryland. You knew that I am Roman Catholic. You were aware that I knew the contents of the message…"

"Ah well, I have spent some time in the Chesapeake region and that subtle twang of yours is an inflection found only in that area." He paused to adjust the brim of his hat as the sun had just found its way through a break in the trees. "Having determined that you are from Maryland, it would be reasonable to assume that you are a Papist but your medallion solidified the notion. In that awful heat yesterday you left the top of your shirt unbuttoned and when you leaned forward to eat I could easily see the St. Michael charm upon your neck-chain. He is the patron saint of battle, no?" He shook his head, "I cannot commend you for belief in such idolatry. But of course I should not criticize-- To each his own."

Shelby digested everything his companion had said and it all fell into place so simply. Hastily he interjected, "But how did you ascertain that I knew what was in the message?"

Mr. Fox let loose with that silent chuckle of his. "*You* betrayed yourself, there. You intently watched the packet as I pulled it toward me across the table and then your gaze shot up to my face and your expression was one of earnest inquiry. It was obvious that you were longing to see my reaction to the message... Ergo you must have been privy to the contents."

The captain considered the explanation. He shook his head in wonderment. "You have unique gifts, Mr. Fox. So, are you a Quaker then?" he reiterated his earlier query.

The man seemed to be weighing the question and a pained look clouded his face. "To a certain degree," he finally said. "Here is the stream. Remember to unpack your pistols while we're letting our mounts drink."

The pair traveled onward until the last vestige of dusk began to give way to the night. They had just emerged from a wood into a large meadow that gradually climbed into a shallow hill when Mr. Fox reined his horse to a halt.

"Ahh, the Lord has provided us a fine dinner!" he said as he dismounted. With complete fluidity of motion, he spun his rifle from his back to an off-hand shooting position. Shelby peered off into the dwindling light in the direction of his companion's aim, but saw absolutely nothing of value in the encroaching gloom. Nonetheless, Fox fired quickly and immediately began to reload with the rapid precision of one experienced in combat.

"There is a spring just beyond the tree-line that side of the field," he said, motioning off to their left. "Be a good lad and

25

ride up and grab that game. Meet me over by the spring. We'll encamp there for the night."

Shelby's confused expression was barely perceivable in the gathering darkness. "Game?" he asked.

"Atop the hillock over there," he replied, pointing with his ramrod in the direction of the far end of the field. "Hurry now Captain or you'll have trouble finding it, night is falling quickly." With that he shouldered his firearm and led his horse away toward the tree-line.

Shelby spurred his pony in compliance, although he thought that Mr. Fox may be a bit touched in the head. The top of the hillock was more than three hundred yards away. "Hitting a buck at that distance in broad daylight would take skill. He must have seen an apparition," he laughed to himself. After all, he possessed excellent eyesight and he had seen absolutely nothing in the direction of Fox's shot.

He scanned the ground when he reached the spot, chuckling at the absence of a fallen deer. However his horse reared slightly, as if it were avoiding stepping on something. Shelby climbed down from his saddle to find the limp body of a large, nearly decapitated hare. He stared at the carcass in disbelief. Finally shaking himself from his astonishment, he tossed the rabbit across his horse's neck in front of his saddle horn, remounted and trotted off in the direction Mr. Fox had indicated.

"Over here, Captain," a disembodied voice softly called from the shadows of the woods. Shelby followed the sound and came upon a hollow illuminated by a campfire. The depression dropped several feet below the level of the surrounding ground, making the fire invisible unless one were staring down into the declivity. A shallow stream gurgled from beneath the exposed roots of a large spruce tree a few feet from an open bedroll.

"You can leave your horse over there," he pointed across the hollow, grabbing up the dead hare.

26

Shelby found Fox's own mount unsaddled and bit removed, loosely tethered to a maple sapling. He followed suit with his own horse and laid out his own bedroll to one side of the campfire and seated himself upon it. By the time he had done so, Mr. Fox had already expertly skinned the rabbit and had it roasting above the flames.

"This hollow would act as a suitable pen for the horses without tying them, but we don't want to get trod upon in our sleep," he said, adjusting the meat slightly. "I provisioned us with some salted pork and hardtack before we left the Twin Oaks, but there is nothing like a fresh hare!" He smacked his lips emphatically.

Shelby's mouth began to water as the aroma wafted toward him. "Mr. Fox, that was an astounding shot! And for someone dependant upon spectacles no less!" He slapped his thigh to accentuate his disbelief.

The man across the fire laughed noiselessly. "When the Lord encumbers us with one defect, he often gifts us in another way as compensation. My sight is strained at close range but I assure you Captain, I have an uncommon acuity at distance."

Shelby laughed. "I should say so! You should be serving with Daniel Morgan's riflemen!" The captain saw the Mona Lisa smirk as the firelight danced across Fox's face. It looked as though he was going to respond to this comment but hesitated and buttoned his lip.

A few moments later Fox said, "Be a good fellow and fill our canteens at the spring, will you, Captain?"

"Certainly," he replied, retrieving the items and completing the deed. He reached down and scooped up handfuls of the water and bathed his face and neck. The liquid was refreshingly cool after such a long day. By the time he returned, his companion had halved the hare and Shelby's portion awaited him, smoking upon the end of a sharpened sassafras sprig.

27

"That was delicious," Shelby said, tossing the remaining bones into the fire and reclining on his bedroll. The cook merely smiled back as he laid another log upon the blaze and lay back upon his own blanket.

"What do you think of this McCrea business, Mr. Fox?" the captain asked, as much to engage in some companionable conversation as out of genuine curiosity over their mission.

"It's too early to say. I am sure that most of the locals believe that the Indians massacred the woman and are presently joining the militia to protect their homesteads." He stared vacantly into the fire as if the thought of an Indian attack stirred some deep and distant reflection.

"Then our assignment is of little consequence," Shelby pondered, chewing on a blade of grass.

"No, I think not, Captain. What the men around Fort Edward conclude is not the same as an official position of your army or our young government. The locals' conjecture may temporarily help in the fight against Burgoyne, but if General Washington or Congress state unequivocally that the British are allowing such savagery; I suspect many more will join the cause throughout the states—and General Alexander was right; they should not say so if it is not true or they will undermine the cause itself."

Shelby smiled impishly before saying, "You seem to impart a great deal of power to the revolution's ideals, Mr. Fox."

"As do you, Captain. Was it not the principles this war was founded upon that led you to join the rebellion?"

"How do you conclude that, Mr. Fox?" he smiled, intrigued by another display of the man's deductive skills.

"Many a young man like yourself has joined this war, and as in past wars, the usual motivation for those your age is a sense of adventure and the personal glory they feel warfare will bring. However, factors indicate that you are less of a thrill-seeker than an idealist."

28

"How so?"

"You could have chosen to fight on either side in this conflict and if adventure or grandeur was your primary goal, the sensible thing to do would be to side with the King's forces. The world gives this rebellion little chance of success, and should the Continental forces lose, an officer in that army may well be executed as a traitor. Fighting for His Majesty however would provide all of the thrilling hazards yet with a much greater prospect for victory and reward."

"Additionally," he continued, "I observed at the tavern that you recognized the title of my little volume. You read Greek. You are an educated fellow. This and your position on General Alexander's staff, furthers the fact that you are not only learned, but valued for your intellect," He tapped his temple with a forefinger. "You are in this fight for its visionary prospects."

Shelby laughed. "You are correct as usual, Mr. Fox. My ire first began to rise when the crown tried to oppress the New Englanders with the Coercive Acts. I could not believe a benevolent monarch could treat his subjects with such cruelty. However, once I read *Common Sense*, I became convinced that the true nature of a government should derive from the will of the people not arbitrary bloodlines of a so called 'sovereign.' So, I joined the fight for independence."

"You had more foresight than some of our leaders," he laughed silently. "They did not decide that we should be independent until a half year after Mr. Paine's monograph had been circulated."

"Yes, well I didn't get my hands on a copy until June of last year so I am not as astute as you believe me to be," he smiled back. "You give much credence to ideals Mr. Fox, yet I find it curious that you have chosen to eschew those of your faith by supporting a side in this war," he said mischievously. Shelby had meant the comment as a humorous jibe but regretted saying it when the flickering shadows of the firelight revealed a troubled look upon Fox's face.

"Perhaps *I am* a hypocrite," he responded in a somber tone. "I certainly have committed my share of sins... But Quakers declare a tolerance for the beliefs of others and that each person possesses an 'inner light' whereby God speaks to that individual directly without need of an intermediary such as a priest or reverend to interpret his will. Aren't these notions the same as the ones behind the revolution?" his voice became more animated. "You just dismissed the divine right of kings by professing that each man has the right to a voice in his own government." He paused, tossing a small stick into the fire. "And you must concede that all efforts short of armed rebellion have fallen short in trying to achieve these goals." The usually composed nature of the man had wavered, and Shelby detected that he was tormented by a deep moral discord.

The young man was aware of course that there were "fighting Quakers;" those who had chosen to take part in the war. He even had had some association with the most prominent of these; General Nathaniel Greene in whose company he had been a number of times. However this man was different. Greene had been expelled by the Quakers and showed no remorse over the banishment. His ardor for military life was whole-hearted and enthusiastic where Shelby's recent acquaintance was apparently conflicted and troubled.

The captain felt a sudden sympathy for the man and now regretted holding back part of his narrative at the tavern. "Mr. Fox, I must tell you, although General Alexander appeared to have no qualms with the decision to bring you into this matter, Colonel Williams was not enthused. He was concerned about your independent nature."

Fox's casual air returned, his crooked smirk driving the clouded expression from his face. "Yes, well generally

30

speaking, soldiers are mistrustful of those who refuse to take an oath, and an oath is something that a Quaker cannot abide."

"He expressed that you might not follow orders," he continued, feeling a need for further penitence.

"And rightly so." Mr. Fox read the shocked expression upon Shelby's face and his shoulders shook in silent laughter. "Captain, remember when you tried to justify the manner in which you had overheard the discussion between the colonel and General Alexander? You had been ordered to sit in the anteroom, and as a soldier you were obligated to follow that order despite the fact that you knew the right thing to do would have been to remove yourself or to close the door." His blue-gray eyes stared into the flames as if musing over some past reminiscence. "Colonel Williams knows all too well that I *will* *not* follow an order if I think it is not the right thing to do."

Chapter 4

Shelby awoke with a start. The fog of sleep still hung over him and it was a full half minute before he realized where he was. There was no moon and the canopy of trees obscured all but a few twinkling stars. The only light was the orange glow of embers that radiated from what had once been their campfire. Lazily, the captain peered over at the bedroll of his companion. He rubbed his eyes to be sure they were not deceiving him but now he was certain-- Mr. Fox had vanished.

The man's blanket remained, his rifle lying neatly alongside. He could also make out the gray form of his horse across the dell. "He has probably just gone to relieve himself," Shelby thought, rolling over. Although eager to slide back into unconsciousness, he could not help but lie awake, waiting for Fox to return like the proverbial 'other shoe to drop.' Five minutes passed, then ten. Concern began to creep into Shelby's mind. After twenty minutes had elapsed, apprehension had a firm grip on the young officer. He was now fully awake, straining his ears to hear any movement in the woods above the cacophony of nocturnal insects and the gentle gurgle of the spring.

Suddenly, close to his left ear he heard, "Don't be alarmed, Captain."

Shelby's reclining body gave a startled jump as he reached for one of his pistols. Almost instantly however, the voice registered as that of Mr. Fox. The man slid past Shelby and over to the spring.

The captain breathed an audible sigh of relief. "You surprised me, Mr. Fox."

"I beg pardon, I had not intended to do so," he returned, as he pulled both a large knife and a tomahawk from his belt and began to wash them in the stream.

Fox was back upon his bedroll in a few moments. Shelby had noticed the knife prior but was taken aback by the Indian weapon. "Where did you find *that?*" he asked, pointing to the sinister implement.

"It is mine," he replied, rolling over. "There was a noise in the forest that bore investigation. I did not want to wake you if it turned out to be nothing," he said with a yawn.

"It was nothing, then?" Shelby spoke to the man's back.

"It was not a war party, which was my chief concern, but a puma can be just as dangerous to sleeping man."

Assuming Fox had scared it off Shelby asked with a tinge of concern, "How do you know that it won't return?"

The man's back shuddered in an inaudible chuckle. "Because I split its skull nearly in two."

The sense of shock had not yet left the young man when the sound of steady breathing indicated that Fox was again asleep. Shelby however lay awestruck. He was amazed that his partner had noiselessly appeared beside him moments before, but even that feat paled considerably in comparison to stalking a panther at night and dispatching it at arm's length--- without a sound of the encounter reaching his ears. "Perhaps he was raised by the Iroquois," he joked to himself as he struggled to shake off his astonishment and return to sleep.

The pair continued their journey the next morning through alternating farm fields, forests and orchards. They were still more than a day's travel from the American forces encamped at Stillwater some twenty-five miles south of Fort Edward.

"You know Mr. Fox, I would not follow an order I found to be immoral." Shelby broke their silent ride. Fox's comments the previous day had lingered in his mind and his irritation had built at what he figured to be a condescending, and somewhat offensive insult to himself and his profession.

Fox shook his head. "I did not mean to slight you, Captain. I do not question your integrity or your dedication to Christian values. I was merely illustrating the difference between us-- and justifying your colonel's apprehension."

Shelby had wanted to believe that Fox had not meant to cast aspersions upon him, so his explanation was readily accepted, however his interest was piqued at the paradox Mr. Fox had placed himself in by supporting armed conflict while opposing the concept of a chain of command. "Do you feel as though all soldiers should evaluate each and every order before carrying them out?"

The other man did not hesitate with his answer, inferring that he had previously reasoned out this question. "No. An army could not function if that were the case. Soldiers must put their faith in their commanders." He chuckled to himself before continuing, "If every Continental soldier followed my example this war would have been lost long ago. However," he continued, "just as soldiers have obligated themselves to obeying orders, those of us who have not enlisted are breaching no compact by thinking for ourselves."

That night the pair found hospitable lodgings at an inn. Shelby enjoyed the opportunity to lubricate his parched throat with some ale and fill his stomach with a stew that if not excellent, was certainly above average. Mr. Fox seemed to enjoy the meal as well, but was true to his Quaker roots by avoiding any spirits and confining himself again to tea. They sat at a quiet table away from prying ears but getting Mr. Fox to engage in conversation was a chore as the man had assumed his more erudite persona. The thin eyeglasses were again perched upon his nose as he lost himself in the leather-bound volume once more.

34

"Mr. Fox," he gently interrupted. "What are we to do when we get to the Stillwater encampment?" In contrast to his normal fashion, the man did not ignore the question until he had concluded his page but answered without looking up.

"The situation will dictate our actions," he stated curtly.

The captain was puzzled by the response. "You mean you do not have a plan on how to proceed with this investigation?"

This time Fox waited until he finished reading and then addressed Shelby more directly. "I have several," he said, taking a sip of tea. "However I simply cannot tell you what avenue will be followed until I know where Burgoyne's army is or who is in our encampment."

"Who is in our encampment?" Shelby repeated quizzically.

"Yes. This McCrea woman lived with a brother serving in the Continental militia. I would very much like to speak with him. If however, he is not with our forces at Stillwater that might not be possible. I would also like to talk to others who knew the girl and it is likely that at least some of those present are from the Fort Edward area."

The captain's brow creased in thought but he dared not ponder for any duration lest Fox return to his book. Quickly he blurted, "Why should you interview those who knew her? Aren't we to ascertain who it was that killed her?"

"Indeed. However it would be helpful to know what her feelings were about the war and how she was regarded by her neighbors." He took another taste of tea. "She was engaged to a Loyalist; but were her own sympathies with the crown as well or was her attachment merely romantic and devoid of politics? If she favored the King, it is indeed peculiar that Indians scouting for the British would kill her. Might local Patriots have resented her affiliation with a Tory and thus shot her down?" His rhetorical questions tumbled atop one another. "Remember the British claim that she was slain by *our* militia."

35

Shelby thought over the situation. "Being betrothed to a Loyalist and yet residing with a Patriot certainly muddies any speculation about loyalties..." he said, scratching his chin.

"It hints that she was neutral in her politics, but this lack of clarity necessitates that we speak with those who knew her to formulate some circumstantial foundations."

"No one is neutral in this conflict," Shelby muttered. "Anyone who claims to be unaligned is merely a member of the third side in this war; the self-interested."

Fox observed that the mention of neutrality had touched a nerve with the young officer and the Mona Lisa smile flitted across his face. He removed his spectacles and began to nibble pensively on one earpiece as he narrowed his eyes at the man seated across the table from him.

"Captain, I suspect that the St. Michael's pendant you wear was the gift of someone who worried over you going to war, and probably tried to dissuade you from enlisting. A sweetheart?" He removed the earpiece from his mouth and gestured toward Shelby with the glasses. "No, a mother or sister, I believe."

The young man was neither amazed nor impressed as he had previously been at Mr. Fox's deductive skills. Rather, the resentment he let slip moments before still lingered, distracting his thoughts homeward. "It was from my sister, Catherine. She is sixteen. My mother died several years back."

"And your father... Was he as unsettled by your enlistment as your sister?"

"He was indeed unsettled, but not over my safety," he grunted. "My father's name," Shelby continued with some disgust, "carries weight because he is a prosperous merchant and through his years of business dealings has connections to important men on both sides in this war. However he refused to help me get a commission, fearing that it might compromise his ability to sell supplies to the British army. You see, he intends to provision whomever he is able, whether their allegiance is to the King or to liberty."

"And yet he is no Tory," Fox added, trying to diminish the young man's anger.

"I wish that he were," Shelby flashed back. "At least then he would have a conviction to something other than gluttony. Had he exerted his influence I would have been commissioned by the state legislature or Congress. Instead, I was forced to enlist. If his refusal to aid me were based on allegiance to the King I would not have liked it, but at least I could have respected his decision."

"You said that you were at Long Island?" Fox asked.

"Yes."

"Major Gist's troops?" Fox furthered, referring to the unit of Marylanders.

"Yes."

Mr. Fox's eyebrows raised in admiration for he knew what that unit had endured and accomplished in the battle. General Alexander's brigade had been cut off from their route of withdrawal. A full British division under General Cornwallis stood between the Patriots and the safety of the American lines in Brooklyn. Gist's Marylanders valiantly attacked the enemy head on to cover the retreat of their comrades. By the following morning only ten of the two hundred and fifty Marylanders had made it to Brooklyn, the remainder having been killed or captured. He deduced that Captain Shelby must have been one of those few. "It is little wonder Alexander wanted to retain the service of this man," Fox thought to himself. "He personally witnessed Shelby's valor in helping to save his troops."

Fox was pensive for a moment. "Of course Captain, had your father secured you a position, you would have probably been commissioned a Lieutenant Colonel. However, I have seen far too many officers appointed only due to their political connections. I don't doubt their patriotism but their lack of experience has cost the lives of the men under them. Captains are usually elected by their peers. Did your fellows choose you?"

"Yes, after our first engagement when our captain was killed."

"Your status exemplifies two of the principles for which we are fighting: the elected will of the common man and meritocracy. If your father had acted on your behalf, you would have compromised those ideals. Instead you have earned your rank."

Shelby appreciated his companion's attempt to assuage his resentment, but the usually astute Quaker had missed the mark if he believed the young man was most irritated by his lesser grade. "What troubles me, Mr. Fox is that my own father should sit in that gray realm of opportunistic neutrality and refuse to throw in his lot. His own friend, Samuel Chase chose not to act with such cowardly caution."

"Mr. Chase signed the Declaration of Independence, did he not?"

"Yes. He, like so many other successful gentlemen put their fortunes on the line, while others like my father…" his teeth clenched, unable to finish the sentence.

Mr. Fox had no further words of consolation to offer as he shared the young man's commitment to the doctrines upon which this war was based and had himself compromised more than commercial affluence for the cause. Rather than affirm Shelby's resentment with any comment he might allow himself to make, he returned to his book.

The morning sun shone brightly upon the two travelers as they continued on the last leg of their journey. The pair had passed to the west of Albany the day before but had since set a northeasterly course that had brought them along the western

38

bank of the Hudson River, which they planned to follow northward to the American headquarters.

"We have drawn the interest of someone," Mr. Fox stated.

Captain Shelby had been lost in his own thoughts and the news startled him. "What's that you say?" he asked, looking around and into the woods that bordered them on the left.

Fox nodded in the direction ahead of them and to the west. "That promontory of rock on yonder hillside. Watch, when he moves you will see the reflection of sunlight from the lens of his spyglass."

Shelby followed his companion's directions, examining the granite formation that jutted from the wooded mountain about a mile ahead of them and within moments he did indeed notice a reflective flash. "We're still too far from Stillwater to encounter the pickets wouldn't you say?"

"Yes. And no forage party would be looking for supplies up there," Fox quipped. "It's possible that it is some paranoid homesteader or self-formed militia company determined to protect their homes."

As they continued onward, Shelby's focus remained on the surroundings and he kept a curious vigil on the mountainside as they passed it. The river gurgled passively on their right but the woods along the left side of the road might be hiding potential danger. Mr. Fox appeared unconcerned, but even he stole furtive glances to and fro and occasionally appeared to be straining his hearing at some phantom sound.

Rounding a bend, they spied two riders on the road ahead. The men were at least a half a mile away, but they were travelling toward Fox and Shelby.

"Do you suppose these gentlemen were the ones observing us?" Shelby asked. "Gentlemen" was a generous description. Even at the extended distance it was evident that the pair were poorly dressed country folk.

"I don't see a spyglass upon either, but of course it could be in one of their bags. They are armed, though." Mr. Fox informed, his keen vision performing a service.

As the pair drew closer, Shelby noticed the smooth bore muskets that each had provocatively in hand, resting across the saddle before him.

"It is probably nothing," Fox whispered, "but be ready nonetheless." Mr. Fox had quietly removed his tomahawk from a saddle bag and slid it into his belt at the small of his back, obscuring it from the view of the approaching men. The captain knew that his partner's rifle was primed and loaded as were his own pistols. He adjusted his baldrick to be sure that he had easy access to his sword.

When the men were fifty feet or so away, they stopped and appeared to be waiting for the Patriots to approach. Shelby's palms began to sweat. He was not nervous, but apprehension began to build as a sixth sense told him that trouble impended. He glanced over at Mr. Fox who continued to lead his horse onward albeit at a slow and wary gait.

Fox adjusted his hat, obscuring his mouth with his forearm in the process. "If I dismount, these two are yours," he hissed. "Hello, friends," he boomed congenially as they reached the men blocking the road. Shelby's alert eye noticed that the men's weapons were half-cocked.

The two groups were now no more than ten feet apart. "Mornin'," one of the ruddy faced men replied. "Nice to see that blue coat," he said to Shelby. "You headed up to Stillwater?"

"Indeed we are," Fox returned. "We are overdue, so if you wouldn't mind stepping aside, we'll be on our way."

"Yeah, I say, it sure is nice to see that blue coat," the man repeated, in a suspiciously loud voice.

Shelby heard a rustle behind them and Fox tumbled instantly from the right side of his saddle as two more men jumped into the roadway just to their rear. The captain immediately comprehended the strategy of the ambush and crossing his arms, drew both pistols from his belt. The man to his right fumbled with the hammer of his musket, trying to bring it back to firing position but his hand slipped and it fell, requiring him to re-cock the mechanism. The other however fired hastily without bringing the gun up to his shoulder. The ball ripped a hole in the sleeve of the captain's coat. Almost simultaneously Shelby fired the pistol in his left hand at the man who had shot at him and the one in his right at the other assailant whose horse had staggered to the side of the trail while the bushwacker fought the hammer back into position. The weapon in Shelby's left hand found its mark, the ball passing through the man's chest. The man's horse reared, flipping the limp body backward over its hindquarters. The second man fell from his horse as well and tumbled roughly down the embankment toward the river.

At the same time as Shelby's fight, Mr. Fox engaged the two men who had attempted to surround them from the rear. As he had rolled from his saddle, Fox expertly spun his rifle to a firing position and from one knee shot from underneath his horse at one of the attackers. His aim was true and the lead passed through the bottom of the man's jaw up into his brain, killing him instantly. However, the impact of the bullet caused the man's finger to tighten on the trigger of the shotgun he carried, letting off the full blast into Fox's mount. The distance was no more than seven feet and the buckshot tore through the beast's thigh and ribs. The severely wounded animal fell sideways, rolling onto Fox's legs. Pinned, he desperately grabbed at the tomahawk at his back as the final highwayman came around the fallen horse, raising his musket to fire. Fox could not free the weapon, and made a frantic grab for the hunting knife at his hip. Before he could remove it from its sheath however the explosion of musket-fire rocked the air.

Fox's hand still gripped the handle of his knife as the ruffian in front of him fell backward. The trapped man looked over his shoulder to see the figure of Captain Shelby emerge through the smoke discharged by the musket he held in his hands. After his second opponent had fallen down the embankment, Shelby had grabbed up his weapon in time to save his companion.

The face of Mr. Fox wore an expression of disbelief as would be expected for one who had just a moment before believed it to be his last. However his mouth quickly curled into that familiar sideways grin. "You know, Captain. I too am glad that you passed that little test at the tavern."

Shelby returned his smile and helped drag him free of his fallen horse. Fortunately Fox was uninjured. The animal was still alive, but lame and suffering. "Are you alright, Captain?" he asked, pointing to the tear in his sleeve.

"Yes, I'm fine. It just creased the material."

Fox nodded in relief. "Might I borrow one of your pistols?" he asked, sadly staring at his tormented horse. Shelby reloaded the weapon and handed it over. Fox stroked the pony's head affectionately and then mercifully ended the animal's suffering.

"Captain, go through the saddle bags of those men and see if there is anything of interest." Shelby complied as Mr. Fox rifled the pockets of the three corpses.

"Ah ha!" Shelby exclaimed. "Here is the spyglass." He picked through the remaining items but found only some ammunition, flints, and tobacco. "I suppose that was their game; to spy travelers upon the road and then fall upon them at this spot."

"I don't think robbery was their motive, Captain." He heard Fox say.

Shelby stepped around the horse and saw that his companion had not only turned the men's pockets inside out and unfastened their clothing, but he had also removed their shoes. "I found this in this one's boot," he stated, handing the captain a folded piece of paper. Shelby examined the article and was stunned by its contents. Upon the page was a written description of both himself and Mr. Fox.

"Someone would rather we not pursue our investigation," Fox said grimly.

Shelby was dumbfounded. "I cannot believe this! Who would possibly know our mission? Or if they did discover our assignment, why resort to two more murders in order to prevent us from carrying it out?"

"A person or persons who are desperate..." Fox replied, scratching his chin. "I wonder if these men are hired guns or were personally involved in the McCrea affair. Where is the fourth one?"

Shelby was lost in thought so it took a moment for Mr. Fox's question to register. "Oh. He fell down the embankment after I shot him."

Fox walked over to the area where the man had fallen from his horse and stared down the rocky expanse. "I don't see a body. You stay here with the horses while I go for a look." He skidded off down the fifty feet of loose stone and scrub pine to the water's edge. The captain peered curiously down at his partner as Fox stooped to examine the ground at the water's edge. In less than five minutes he was back up the hill.

"There is a blood trail all the way down to the water. Whether you mortally wounded him or he made his escape downriver I cannot say. But one thing is certain: this thing runs deeper than I had originally anticipated."

Chapter 5

With some effort the pair had dragged the deceased horse to the edge of the embankment and shoved it over so as to keep the roadway clear. Captain Shelby would have been content to do the same with the corpses of the three cut-throats but Mr. Fox had insisted upon burying them; albeit only under piles of the loose rocks that littered the roadside. The Quaker prayed over the site for a minute before returning to where Shelby stood holding the horses. Fox picked the better of the two formerly ridden by their attackers and replaced the saddle and bags with his own, which were of a much higher caliber. He secured the assailant's accoutrements to the other horse and the men assumed the road once more, trailing the third pony behind them.

"I know that Catholics believe that the dead should be given ecclesiastical rites and interred in consecrated ground," Fox stated as they rode along. "The later of course was not possible but although I am no priest, I tried to satisfy the former."

Shelby grunted. "You do not have to placate my religious beliefs, Mr. Fox. I suppose you will find me callous, but I wouldn't waste any effort trying to do right by those would-be murderers."

"Yes," Fox said pensively. "It is hard to feel sympathy for those bent on such a malevolent task." He paused. "I won't preach to you Captain, but when you have the chance, reflect upon the phrase from the Pater Noster: *...forgive us our trespasses as we forgive those who trespass against us...*"

Even if Shelby had the inclination to relate the phrase from the *Our Father* to the men they had just left buried behind them,

44

his brain once again gravitated to the enigmatic, reluctant warrior beside him who had dispatched the assassin without hesitation and appeared to have not the slightest bit of regret over his actions. Yet, he showed concern over the souls of those who had been bent on murdering them.

"Mr. Fox, why did you suspect an ambush?" the captain asked, curious about the man's methods.

"Suspect is too strong a word, Captain. I have learned that when something does not seem right, it probably isn't. I did not like the slow gait of those riders, and I especially did not care for the fact that they stopped some distance ahead. It felt to me as if they wanted to encounter us at that exact spot. I could conjure no reason for this that did not involve skullduggery." Fox shot his companion that crooked smirk. "My thinking was merely presumptively cautious."

"Do you not find it shocking that those men were sent to kill us?" Shelby asked, returning to the thoughts he had had following the discovery of the paper in the man's boot.

"It certainly is curious to say the least. I suspect that we would have a much clearer picture if we had been able to question at least one of them. They were acting on orders, that much is definite. But it is also hard to imagine that they were who they appeared to be."

"How do you mean?"

Fox lifted his hat and wiped the sweat from his forehead with his sleeve. "Those fellows were made up to be local bandits, and it was supposed to look as if we had fallen victim to them. It is not uncommon for travelers to suffer such a fate in the neutral ground. Yet, at least the one I killed, perhaps all four, were imposters."

"You mean to say that even though they were put on to us, they were not neighborhood brigands out for plunder?"

"It is possible that whoever gave them our description told them we carried valuables-- but it is unlikely that local hayseeds

45

would be literate. No, as I said, I suspect that at least one, perhaps all, were only disguised as highwaymen."

Shelby ruminated over the written description found upon the man Fox had shot. "Who do you believe them to be, then?"

Fox's brow furrowed. "That I cannot say. But nefarious forces are at work, to be sure."

The pickets and outlying patrols acknowledged the uniform and rank of Captain Shelby and did not molest them as they approached the encampment. It was early evening as they ambled through the rows of tents and the aroma of the cooking fires reached their noses and tempted their stomachs. Shelby asked directions to the commanding general's headquarters and were directed to a house a short distance away. Upon reaching their destination they dismounted and lashed their horses to the post.

"Should we mention the bushwackers?" Shelby asked quietly.

"No, I think not," Fox returned. "We need to formulate a more solid foundation in these matters before we are too trusting of anyone, even General Gates."

Shelby approached a guard outside the door and returned the man's salute. "Is General Gates present, Private?"

"Not yet, sir. He has yet to arrive; General Schuyler is still in command."

"Oh. Well is General Schuyler inside?"

"Yes, sir."

"I am Captain Shelby and this is Mr. Fox, we have been sent from General Washington's headquarters and must confer with the general. May we enter?" The man was obviously impressed at the mention of the commander-in-chief and stood aside.

Inside the house officers were bustling about, analyzing maps and sending aides off in this direction or that. Shelby found a major and repeated what he had told the sentry.

46

"May I have a look at your orders, Captain?" the major asked.

Sheepishly Shelby replied. "I have no written orders... Our mission is a delicate one. I am sure that General Schuyler was informed that we would be arriving."

The major's face showed displeasure at the unorthodoxy of the situation but dared not dismiss the pair on the possibility that the general was indeed expecting them. He led them to an anteroom and disappeared through a door, closing it behind him. In a moment he was back, and Fox and Shelby were ushered inside where they found the general and a lieutenant colonel seated at a table eating their dinner, an attendant posted dutifully along the wall.

Schuyler did not rise when the two entered but merely waved them in. Shelby had never met Schuyler, but he knew of him. The General had served in the British army during the French and Indian War and was from one of the most prominent and wealthy families in New York. He had a mansion in Albany, but also a large country estate at Saratoga. Schuyler was known as a savvy businessman owning mills and lumber operations, even building a fleet of ships to move his lumber down the Hudson for projects in Manhattan. He had been a delegate to the Continental Congress, but had left that body after accepting a commission as Major General, returning home to New York to head up the Northern Department.

Captain Shelby removed his cocked hat; however this respectful gesture did not occur to his unconventional companion until he witnessed Shelby hang his tricorne upon a hook of the stand in the corner. Then, Fox followed suit though more for the sake of comfort than any deference to the rank of the diners.

"Reynolds," the general said to the attendant, "Get two more plates for these men. Have a seat," he invited them, albeit without much congeniality in his tone. "I take it you're hungry?"

"Yes sir," Shelby answered for both of them, "We've been on the road all day."

Schuyler grunted in reply. "This is Colonel Varick." The colonel merely nodded a greeting. "I take it you are Shelby and Fox?" the general finished, continuing with his meal. Shelby found it curious that the general appeared totally indifferent to the peculiarity of his partner.

"Yes sir," the captain replied but offered nothing further as the attendant returned and placed a generous plate of beef, potatoes and corn in front of each man. He then filled Shelby's glass from a bottle of wine. He went to do the same to Fox's, but the Quaker covered its mouth with his hand.

"I'll just have some of this water, if you don't mind," he said. Without waiting to be served, he grabbed up the pitcher himself and filled his vessel.

"Leave us, Reynolds," the general ordered. The man gave a respectful nod and disappeared through the door, closing it as he left.

"So, you're up here to investigate the McCrea girl's murder?" Schuyler commented between bites.

"Yes sir," returned the captain.

"Colonel Varick has been apprised of your mission," the general nodded toward his dinner-mate. "He's the only one in camp besides me who knows why you're here. You can go to him if you need anything. I'm leaving the colonel here to keep an eye on Gates," he said contemptuously. "I'm not going to have that conniving popinjay screw up all we've accomplished." He took a sip of his wine, apparently to calm himself. "If Gates thinks he's outfoxed me by grabbing hold of this command, he's mistaken," the general vented cooly. "I'll vindicate myself, you can be certain of that and Varick here will make sure that I get a clear picture of what Gates is up to while I'm away."

Shelby had heard enough in the presence of General Alexander and Colonel Williams to know that Schuyler and

Gates disliked one another and that each had been using all of their respective political connections to discredit the other's character and abilities. Yet he was surprised at Schuyler's open disrespect in front of strangers.

The general continued, "So even when Gates assumes this command, Colonel Varick will still be at your disposal. He will inform the general of your mission although I doubt he will care much, unless it can contribute some accolades to him personally."

Shelby dismissed the jibe and shifted the focus away from their assignment, curious about the present state of affairs. "Sir, if I may ask, how are things here? General Alexander expressed concern over the prospect of three British armies converging on this position."

"Three? Make that two." The general stated curtly. "We've received word that Howe will not be coming north from Manhattan. It appears that he intends to head south instead."

Shelby smiled. "That is excellent news! That certainly throws an impediment into General Burgoyne's plan."

Schuyler laughed. It was the first time his face had morphed from a scowl. "It's not the only 'impediment' Burgoyne's found, eh Colonel?"

Varick joined Schuyler's mirth adding: "General Schuyler has slowed Burgoyne's progress to a crawl. Practically every tree along the road from Ticonderoga was felled across the trail, making passage all but impossible. We've destroyed every bridge along his planned route, and dammed up a number of streams, flooding much of his path. And the general also ordered the obliteration of any supplies that the Lobsterbacks might have used in the vicinity." The colonel's smile widened. "Burgoyne was forced to cut an entirely new road. He was weeks behind schedule by the time he reached Fort Edward."

Shelby's chest warmed at the news. Whatever criticism General Gates might have about Schuyler, he had certainly taken decisive and effective steps in the face of Burgoyne's advance. "What of St. Leger's army? I know that they were to advance down the Mohawk," Shelby asked, without revealing that he had come by this information unofficially, through overhearing the conversation of General Alexander and Colonel Williams.

Schuyler's scowl returned. "St. Leger is besieging Fort Stanwix some ninety miles northwest of here. Last week a militia unit tried to relieve the fort but was ambushed by his Tories and Indians at Oriskany and turned back. I'm sure you saw all that activity out there," the general pointed to the front of the house with his fork. "I'm preparing to send an expedition to confront St. Leger and relieve Fort Stanwix as we speak."

During this discussion Mr. Fox seemed interested only in his meal and had not even looked up as the military men conferred about the strategic situation. Whether he had been silently absorbing the material or totally indifferent was a mystery.

"General," Fox broke into the conversation for the first time. "The McCrea girl's brother is a militia officer. I would like to speak with him if possible."

"Arrange that, will you, Colonel," Schuyler ordered his subordinate. Varick nodded affirmation as he chewed his potatoes.

The rest of the meal was spent in not unpleasant, if not overly warm conversation. It was evident that the general resented losing the political struggle with Gates and his seething scorn distracted him from any depth of discussion.

"Gentlemen," the general said, rising. "If you will excuse me, I still have much to do in making sure the relief expedition can get underway." He turned to Varick. "Colonel, see to the needs of these men." Shelby saluted, and began to offer his thanks but the surly officer was already on his way out of the door.

Colonel Varick shook his head in a perturbed manner. "He's a good man," he said. "He does not deserve the maligning he has received. Gates had been trying to get a hold of this post for a year. Last September, General Schuyler offered his resignation to Congress and they turned him down. Now, the battle is about to be joined in his backyard and they remove him. It is beyond idiotic. Schuyler is intimately familiar with this area. He knows every hill and ravine. We are about to engage Burgoyne and they bring in a less able man." There was an angry bite in Varick's words. "I don't know if we will be victorious or not under General Gates, but I assure you that more of our men will die due to his unfamiliarity with this terrain."

Shelby sighed. "That may be so. But at least General Schuyler was here to impede Burgoyne thus far or it is unlikely that there would even be an army for General Gates to command," he said, trying to brighten the bitter man's spirits.

"I wish that I were accompanying him to his new post," Colonel Varick returned.

"I admire your loyalty," Mr. Fox interjected. "He must value you a great deal as well," he smirked at the colonel, "to leave you here as his agent."

Varick's sorrowful expression bent into a grin at the backhanded compliment. "Yes, well I suppose I will be able to do him a service by remaining here." He smiled. "Come now and I'll show you to your tent."

"You know," Varick said as they walked along, "the McCrea murder is only the tip of the iceberg. We have had at least two dozen pickets and foragers slaughtered and scalped since the girl's death. Burgoyne's Indians are running wild. They are not only bloodthirsty; they are deranged. We found one soldier not only scalped, but flayed and missing his hands."

"I have no doubt," Mr. Fox replied in a solemn tone, alluding to a first-hand knowledge of such episodes. "But Jane McCrea has become symbolic of such atrocities. Her story is spreading throughout the country and is becoming a recruiting tool for our cause. It is imperative that we find out if it is accurate. As an unsubstantiated tale, it is doing admirable work but Congress cannot come out behind the account if it is untrue." Colonel Varick stopped in front of a large tent befitting an officer. "We were expecting you, so we outfitted this tent for your use. I hope it is satisfactory."

Such accommodations were a true luxury in an army where many slept upon the naked ground. General Schuyler had not revealed whether or not he considered their mission to be of any importance but he obviously respected that they were acting on the orders of the commander-in-chief. The interior held two cots and a table upon which rested a large pitcher of water, ample washbasin and two clay cups. The table had apparently been commandeered from some local home but only two of the several chairs that went with the set were present. An unlit lantern hung from a nail upon the post in the center of the room.

"I hope this is adequate for your needs," Varick said. "Your things are over there." He pointed to a corner of the tent where their effects had been laid. "I've also had a map brought in," he continued, ushering them over to the table to show them the two by three foot chart of the surrounding area. "I don't know how familiar you are with this country…"

"That should be helpful," Shelby acknowledged the gesture appreciatively and stepped over to the table. He scanned the map with interest and the colonel took down the lantern and lit it as the daylight was on the wane.

Mr. Fox gave no indication as to whether or not he was knowledgeable about the locale, merely stating in a somewhat indifferent tone: "Very good, Colonel. About the girl's brother. Can you see if you can scare him up for us?"

"Oh, yes," he returned, with an apologetic tinge in his voice as if he were disappointed in himself for misreading their priorities. The colonel apparently took great pride in the employment of his duties and had assumed that the visitors

52

would prefer to settle in to their lodgings. "I'll see to it immediately," he said and ducked out of the flap.

Fox removed his powder horn and cartridge box and then his hat and coat. He rolled up his sleeves and poured a generous amount of water into the bowl. As the man bathed his face in the cool liquid, Shelby noticed a rather vicious looking scar that ran up his left forearm. Upon finishing, Fox moved over to the pile where his effects lay and retrieved his Greek volume from his saddlebag. "If you wouldn't mind Captain, until the colonel returns, I would like some solitude," he stated matter-of-factly. He placed the lantern upon the table and his spectacles upon his face, took a seat at one of the chairs, and delved into his book. Shelby shrugged his shoulders at the eccentric man and smiled, taking his own turn at the washbasin. Outside a familiar cadence sounded as a drumbeat called the companies for the sunset roll call.

A full two hours had passed since Colonel Varick had left them. If Mr. Fox was bothered by this unusual duration, it did not show as he appeared content in entertaining himself with his reading. Shelby was not so settled. The captain lay upon his cot for some time. Dozing seemed out of the question knowing that the moment Varick returned with their quarry he needed to be fully functional. He spent some of this period studying the map, more to assuage his boredom than to intimately acquaint himself with the surroundings. Shelby cycled through the cot-to map back to cot-circuit no fewer than three times. He began to regard his companion's text with an increasing degree of jealously and had just returned to his bed again when the wayward colonel appeared through the portal.

"Mr. Fox, I am sorry…" Varick began but was forced to arrest himself as the Quaker held up his forefinger.

Shelby crept over to the colonel and said quietly, "Forgive him, sir. He has a rather disagreeable trait in that he refuses to be interrupted when he is reading."

It appeared that Mr. Fox was somewhat more accommodating to the colonel than he had been to Shelby as he only held him at bay until he reached the end of the page as opposed to the chapter.

"What? No Mr. McCrea?" he asked in a tone of mocking reprobation, as he removed his reading glasses.

Varick shook his head. "No, Mr. Fox. I am afraid not. You see, when General Schuyler heard that Howe was not heading this way, he ordered that a unit be dispatched toward Manhattan to ensure that we had not received faulty intelligence. It seems that Colonel McCrea was with that force."

Fox's brows furrowed. "That is unfortunate." Suddenly however the cloud passed. "Ah well! If he returns while we are still here, please direct him to me."

"Certainly, sir. Is there anything else I can do for you at present?"

"What's that?" Mr. Fox had been momentarily lost in thought. "No, no. Thank you, Colonel. Check in with us in the morning, will you?"

After Varick had left, Shelby sighed loudly. "So what are we to do now?"

"Well," Fox returned, moving over to his bunk and rolling back onto it. "Tomorrow I will be leaving for Fort Edward. I need to nose about the McCrea woman's neighborhood a bit."

"*You* will be leaving? What am I to do?" Shelby asked with some indignation in his voice. In addition to lamenting the boredom he envisioned he would endure waiting for Mr. Fox to return, Shelby was actually becoming engrossed in his role as investigator. Despite possessing great discipline, impetuousness now surfaced at the prospect of being left out of a facet of the investigation.

"My dear Captain!" He laughed in that silent manner of his. "I cannot take you. Remember, Fort Edward is behind Burgoyne's lines. If you were to travel there wearing that

54

uniform, before long you would find yourself chained up in one of those dreadful prison ships anchored in New York Harbor."

Shelby opened his mouth to interject, but Fox had apparently read his mind, continuing, "And if you were to change into civilian attire, and you were found to actually be a Continental officer, they would hang you as a spy."

The captain exhaled derisively. "You don't really think I might be recognized?"

"Even Maryland has its Tories and who's to say none of them are with Burgoyne's army? You might run directly into one of your neighbors. No, I won't risk your life over a bit of work that I can accomplish just as easily without your help."

The captain's facial features hardened into a pout. "Well, what am I to do, then?"

"I have a job for you-- which I will explain to you in the morning. Now be a good lad and put out that lantern," he said before lying back with his hands behind his head and closing his eyes.

As Shelby snuffed the light, he was unsure if the sideways grin that now resided upon Fox's face was habitual or if forcing the curious captain to wait until the morrow was a means of amusing himself.

Chapter 6

Shelby blinked groggily. It was still dark; he had no idea of the time. The dryness in his throat caused him to wish for a drink of water. However, the pitcher upon the table was empty and his canteen was across the tent piled alongside their other items. The young man was in that state of heavy exhaustion brought on not so much as a result of the day's activities as from the sudden interruption of a very deep sleep. His limbs felt as if they were made of lead and his head seemed shrouded in a heavy fog. As much as he longed to quench his thirst, the prospect of trudging to the far side of the tent to obtain relief did not appeal to the overly fatigued soldier. He lay in semi-consciousness debating which ailed him more: dehydration or exhaustion. Finally, his parched throat won the argument. Yet his body rebelled at the decision and he had to forcibly thrust himself from his bunk. As he did so, he collided with an object in the gloomy interior. His mind was still foggy, but whatever he had slammed into reeled backward from the impact yet was solid enough to cause Shelby to do the same, causing him to fall back onto his cot. A confused clatter followed as a third object silhouetted itself against the front of the tent and then dissolved into nothingness.

But a moment had passed and he was on his feet again extending a hand to his tent-mate who lay upon his back on the dirt floor. "Mr. Fox, I am sorry, are you alright? I was just getting up for a drink of water. I didn't see you there."

"Did you get a look at him?" Fox asked, dismissing the apology but accepting the helping hand.

"A look at him?" Suddenly the haze of sleep evaporated from the captain's brain. "There was an intruder in our tent!"

"Yes," Fox replied, a hint of glumness in his voice. "I was about to pounce on him."

Shelby took a seat on the edge of his cot. "And I ruined it," the dejected captain stated.

"There is no sense dwelling upon an unintentional accident," the shadow on the other side of the tent said in a brightened tone. "Be a good lad and light the lantern, but stay clear of the doorway. I want to inspect the ground for footmarks."

Mr. Fox crept over to their effects and rummaged through his baggage, returning with an object in his hand. The contrite soldier handed the lamp over to his partner, noticing that he held a magnifying lens. He watched intently as Mr. Fox dropped to his knees and slowly played the light around the front of their tent. At one point he appeared to grab up an object, but Shelby could not see what it was from his present angle. Then the investigator laid himself with his nose but a few inches from the ground and played the convex glass over the area. After a long five minutes of inspection, he placed the lantern and lens upon the table and seated himself upon his own bunk.

"There are footmarks. The man wears about a size eight shoe and has a small triangular chip in the right heel," Fox stated, returning his eyeglasses to their case and depositing them back in his pocket.

"What do you suppose he was after?"

"Murder, I should think," Fox returned, tossing an object onto the cot next to where Shelby sat. The captain looked down at a formidable hunting knife.

Shelby lay awake for some time afterward. However the regular breathing across the tent indicated that this was not the case with his partner. The captain marveled at Fox's apparent ability to sleep soundly while apparently possessing some sixth sense which allowed him to simultaneously stay vigilant. This was the second time he had done so, convincing Shelby that his awareness of the puma had been no mere stroke of luck.

The captain's mind shifted to the prowler. He thought, "General Schuyler said that no one in camp besides Colonel Varick and he knew of our mission. Apparently that is not so. Unless..." He wondered if Mr. Fox had seen enough of the intruder to dismiss Varick as a suspect. He shook his head, disbelieving his own suspicion of the colonel. He simply couldn't conceive that Varick might have any such ill-intent. He had been so sincere in trying to aide them thus far. However, he had to admit to himself that he might be mistaken. After all, he was new to this investigative game. And, Varick had been set up with General Gates as a spy for Schuyler. Perhaps deception was one of his gifts.

At sunup the drums again began to tap and revelry roused the soldiers from their slumber. Shelby had been conditioned by the familiar cadence and despite the uneasy night's sleep, he sprang from his cot. His companion had already replenished their pitcher of water, washed, and dressed. He stood surveying the map upon the table.

"Good morning, Captain," he said cheerfully, as if they had not been nearly murdered just hours before.

"Good morning," replied Shelby as he retrieved his shaving kit from his effects and set about the daybreak rituals of a soldier. "Mr. Fox," the captain said as he peered into a small mirror and began to scrape the blade across his face. "Yesterday the general told us that no one in camp beside Colonel Varick and he knew of our mission. Do you believe General Schuyler was mistaken?"

Fox answered without looking up from the map. "Oh, it is possible. I have found that the higher the rank, the more likely they are to make such declarative statements. Conceit too often is a byproduct of authority. Many officers simply refuse to admit that anything occurs under them of which they are unaware."

Shelby chose his words carefully, uneasy about maligning Varick. "So... Is there anyone in particular you suspect as the intruder?"

"I'm fairly certain of the perpetrator's identity."

The news startled the shaving man into nicking himself. "You are?" he blurted, dabbing the small red crescent upon his chin with a towel.

The left side of Fox's lips angled upward. "It was too dark last night, but this morning I was able to make a more thorough inspection. Look here," he said, walking over to the front of the tent and pointing to the ground. Shelby came over and observed a drop of blood upon the dirt.

"I thought that I knocked into you before you had a chance to strike him."

"You did, but when you collided with me, I banged into him. See here," he pointed to an area next to the drop of blood.

"Where? I don't see anything."

He crouched and indicated a precise spot with the end of the earpiece of his spectacles and then held the magnifying glass over the area. There, appeared a brownish red item no more than a quarter inch in size. "When you slammed into me, and I crashed into that scoundrel, it dislodged that clot. I am not responsible for the man's wound," he declared. "If I am correct, that honor belongs to you."

"To me?" Suddenly Fox's assertion dawned on him. "The ambusher I shot?"

"That is my presumption. But that clot was not formed naturally. Either that fellow had some training in medicine, or he obtained treatment elsewhere. Let us have the colonel send us a boy we can dispatch to see if any of the surgeons in the camp are responsible."

59

"Wait," Shelby asserted. "Why don't we follow the blood trail? It might lead us right to him!"

Fox's shoulders shook in that quiet chuckle of his. "You are getting the hang of this, Captain. But alas, I've already tried that while you were still sleeping. There are a few drops outside the tent, but none beyond that. He must have had the wherewithal to cover the wound with his sleeve or handkerchief as he fled. We should however canvass the sentries. They may have seen something or if we're tremendously fortunate, even captured him as he tried to slip out of camp."

Mr. Fox grabbed a leather pouch from the table and slid the magnifying lens into it. As he did so, Shelby's eyes widened when he saw the name inscribed upon the instrument: *B. Franklin.* Was Mr. Fox acquainted with perhaps the most famous man upon the globe? He was about to pose the very question when Colonel Varick arrived.

The captain's curiosity shifted as he wondered just how much Mr. Fox would reveal about their near miss the night before. And as it turned out, he said nothing of the encounter. Did this mean that he suspected Varick as a conspirator?

"Gentlemen, I've ordered a private to retrieve some victuals for you. He should be here in a few moments."

"Thank you, Colonel," Fox replied. "Would you be able to direct me to the Captain of the Guard?"

"If you don't mind Colonel, I'll just finish with my shaving," Shelby interjected.

"Certainly, Captain." Turning to Fox he replied, "That would be Captain Gower." A soldier appeared at the tent opening, holding a crude plank that served as a tray for some foodstuffs. "Put that on the table there, Private." Varick said to him. Turning back to Fox he continued, "I'll go find Captain Gower while you're eating and bring him back with me."

"Very good Colonel," Fox replied, "But one more thing. Could you leave the private here with us for a moment? I have

60

an errand that I would like him to run," He asked, pulling up a chair to the table even before Varick could reply. If the colonel was curious about either request, he made no show of it.

"Certainly." He turned to the young soldier, "Private, attend to whatever Mr. Fox may need."

With that Varick disappeared on his own errand and Fox told the private to visit each regimental physician and inquire if in the last twelve hours any had treated a civilian for a gunshot wound. As the pair devoured the breakfast, Fox asked, "Isn't this jam delicious? I don't believe I've ever had mulberry jam quite as good."

Shelby had to agree that the preserve was excellent, but he could not relax as much as his companion. His life had been in jeopardy countless times since this war began, but the possibility of death upon the field had never bothered him. Mr. Fox had warned that their endeavor brought with it hazards quite unique from that arena, however he was having difficulty with the fact that they were the targets of unknown foes. Even the ambush had been less dastardly than this recent attempt on their lives. How depraved could a soul be to conspire to murder men in their sleep?

"Captain Gower, this is Captain Shelby and Mr. Fox," Varick introduced.

Gower, a thin, hard looking man exchanged salutes with Shelby but it was Fox who addressed him.

"Captain, we are here at the behest of the commander-in-chief." This was the extent of Fox's explanation which in its brevity gave away no details yet bestowed great authority upon the pair. "How was the watch last night? Anything of significance occur?"

Gower looked pensive for a brief moment. "No, sir. All was quiet," he stated, a faint hint of a German accent upon his voice.

"Thank you, Captain. That will be all," Fox returned. After the guardsman had left them he turned to Varick. "Colonel, I believe that we have troubled you enough at present."

"Alright then. I will be at headquarters," he said, apparently anxious not to fall behind in his regular duties. However he courteously added, "Gentlemen, if you need me to come to you, just order a soldier to fetch me and I will proceed directly. Please do not hesitate if you require anything at all."

A few minutes after Varick had departed, the young private returned. "Sir," Dr. Turner, surgeon for the 8th Massachusetts says that he treated a man like you described yesterday."

"Is that so?" Fox smiled toward Shelby. "Where might we find this Dr. Turner?"

"He and a few of the other doctors have set up a small hospital in a house toward the west end of the encampment. If you head off that-a-way," the young man pointed. "You will eventually find a lane. Across that lane is the hospital. It will be hard to miss."

"Thank you soldier, you are dismissed." Turning to Shelby, Fox said, "I prefer to stretch my legs in the morning anyway, would you care to accompany me, Captain?"

The duo weaved through the rows of tents, past a company drilling in a small green before finding the lane. Across the road the hospital sat languidly. Men and women came and went but their pace was sluggish, their gait unhurried. Shelby was well aware that at times like these, most patients were victims of "camp fever" rather than wounded. But if a battle commenced, this place would lose its lethargy and become as energetic as the field itself.

Behind the house were two barns and a series of other outbuildings, all in use as part of the hospital. Mr. Fox approached a matronly woman as she descended the house's front porch. "Pardon, Miss. Where might we find Dr. Turner?"

She looked him up and down before answering. "Front room, to the left," she curtly stated before continuing on her way. "Charming." Shelby smiled to Mr. Fox, mocking the terse woman.

Inside they found the doctor, an extremely thin man with a hawkish nose and a bald head fringed with red hair. While most of the home had been set aside for the sickliest men, the apartment where they found the physician had been established as an examination room. He acknowledged them but begged a moment and ducked behind a curtain to treat a patient. Despite the low tones, Shelby easily concluded that the man's complaint was of a venereal persuasion. A few minutes later a young soldier emerged from behind the enclosure and skulked off.

"So gentlemen, what ails you?" the doctor asked congenially as he wiped his hands upon a rag, his words thickly coated with a New England accent.

"Oh, it's nothing like that, doctor." Mr. Fox replied, flashing his crooked smirk. "The captain and I have been informed that you recently treated a civilian for a single gunshot wound. It would have been superficial because it did not impair his physical ability to any significant extent."

Dr. Turner finished wiping his hands and tossed the towel over the frame of the curtain. "Yes. The fellow was some farmer from around here somewhere. Apparently the victim of a hunting accident. And you've described it right accurately. It *was* superficial. It was a clean wound; the shot passed clear through the deltoid, er this area here." He pointed to the rounded meaty part of the shoulder. "Missed the bone entirely."

"Could you describe the man, please?" Shelby chimed in.

"Ruddy fellow. Brown hair. Tan clothing."

Fox and Shelby looked at each other in confirmation.

"What, did he steal some rations or something while he was in camp?"

63

"Something like that," Shelby returned. "Thank you, doctor."

Mr. Fox was quiet as they hiked back across the lane. Since Shelby had been enlisted into this partnership he had become ever increasingly intrigued by the man and despite great effort he could not prevent himself from ruminating not only about Fox's past but also about the workings of his mind. He wanted desperately to inquire about his companion's thoughts but was reticent about interrupting his musings.

"Ezra!" a voice called out. "Ezra!" sounded again, and suddenly Fox was shaken from his concentration, looking off in the direction of the cry. Shelby followed his gaze to find a short but stoutly built Negro man in his late twenties advancing from between the tents.

"Josiah?" Fox returned, for once his smile expanded across both sides of his mouth. "Well, I'll be! It is good to see you, my friend!" he said, shaking the man's hand. "How are you?"

"Fine, fine. And yourself?" Josiah replied, smiling.

"Oh, I am well, I suppose. I didn't know that you were stationed with Schuyler."

"I wasn't until two weeks ago when we were brought over from Rhode Island."

Apparently Fox expected the man to next ask what *he* was doing there, so he quickly jumped in. "This is Captain Shelby," he introduced. "We've been sent to do a bit of accounting." The explanation was true, but so overtly vague that Josiah had no difficulty comprehending that he should not press further. "Captain, this is Josiah Strong."

"It is good to meet you," Shelby said, returning the salute thrown up by the lower ranking soldier.

"Likewise," the man smiled. "We are due to drill in a few minutes, so I must be going, but I hope that we will have some time to visit together later. How about this evening? My unit is encamped just over there." He pointed to a section of tents.

64

"I would enjoy nothing more, but unfortunately I have to leave camp for a few days. However, perhaps when I return?"

"I am looking forward to it." He smiled broadly. "We are going to give it to Burgoyne, you wait and see! Again, nice to meet you, Captain." He shook Shelby's hand again and then, losing his familiarity, stood upright and saluted. Shelby returned the salute. "And thank you again, Ezra," he said, turning back toward Mr. Fox. Fox waved off the comment as Josiah headed off toward the green where his comrades were assembling.

The pair resumed walking again and noticing that Mr. Fox was less pensive, Shelby struck up a conversation. "Ezra, is it then?" he smirked.

"Ezra it is. My!" He smiled back. "I don't know your Christian name, Captain. Would you do me the honor of enlightening me?"

"Certainly. But I had assumed that you did know, given your powers of clairvoyance," he laughed. "It is William. By the way," Shelby interjected, "Why did he thank you?"

Fox's face assumed a more serious expression. "I am sure you are aware that back in January of this past year, General Washington issued a general order allowing for the enlistment of free Negroes."

"Yes."

"Well, Josiah was eager to enlist, charmed by the same principles of liberty that drew both you and I to this war. However, a fellow from Delaware contested Josiah's status, claiming that he was a slave who had run away from his household some ten years prior. I helped Josiah acquire a certificate attesting that the gentleman was mistaken and that Josiah was actually a free man."

Shelby was quiet for few strides before asking, "*Was* the man mistaken?"

Fox scratched his chin. "I would say that any man is mistaken if he believes he has the right to own another human being."

The captain was silent again. After several seconds had elapsed he said, "You know, my father owns a half dozen. He sent one of them as a replacement to serve in his place when Congress issued a draft and he tried to substitute one for me as well."

"And how does that sit with you-- owning other people?" There was an edge in Fox's usually easy voice.

"It is my father who owns them, Mr. Fox, not I," the captain stated curtly, unhappy about the assertion that he was in anyway culpable for his father's actions. However he also did not like his partner's judgmental tone and jabbed back, "You know Mr. Fox, Lord Dunmore offered Virginia's slaves their freedom if they agreed to fight for England. If this issue is so pressing to you, you may be on the wrong side."

The normally even-tempered Quaker stopped in his tracks. Fox appeared to be grappling with containing his anger. Shelby thought that perhaps he had crossed the line, but was unapologetic in fending off the critical remark. He stood, waiting for Fox's response.

After a deep breath Fox turned toward the younger man. "Captain, you and I have already discussed the unfortunate reality that some principles must often be compromised to achieve a greater good. I *do* remember Dunmore's proclamation, but I suspect that it was an act of desperation and that if our quest for independence fails it would not be honored. However, if we win this war, I am hopeful that the tenets laid out in our own Declaration of Independence will be brought to fruition, even for the Negro." Fox glowered at Shelby with uncharacteristic fire in his eyes, but the captain gathered that his ire was not so much at him, but a result of a deep-seated angst over an issue that ran so counter to his Quaker ideals.

Fox did not wait for a reply and began walking again. Shelby caught up and strode silently alongside, hoping that without further comment, the conflict would soon be forgotten. He had gauged correctly, for by the time they reached the tent all signs of annoyance had dissipated.

"Captain," Fox said cordially. "I told you that I had a job for you while I was away. Let me explain what I would like you to do." Before Mr. Fox could begin, a noise was heard from outside the tent.

"Mr. Fox? Captain? May I enter?" Colonel Varick's voice sounded from beyond the flaps.

"Certainly, Colonel," Mr. Fox returned.

As the officer entered, both men were taken aback by his disturbed expression.

"What is it, Colonel?" Shelby asked.

"We have just gotten word. Colonel McCrea has been killed."

"Killed?" Shelby echoed. Immediately his mind shifted to military considerations. "Were the reports false? Has Howe pushed out from Manhattan?"

"No. It appears that the reports were accurate and Howe is not coming."

"Did they run into a patrol then?" Shelby followed up.

"No. They encountered neither Redcoat nor Tory." He bit his lip in thought for a moment. "They were returning, and a mere mile from this very camp, when Colonel McCrea was felled by a sniper."

"A sniper?" Shelby repeated.

Mr. Fox jumped in, "Was anyone else hit?"

"No Mr. Fox; that is the odd thing. A single shot killed the colonel as if he were the sole target. As strange as it sounds, it appears to have been an assassination."

Chapter 7

After Varick had left, Shelby turned toward his partner. "Do you think he is correct? Was Colonel McCrea murdered?" he asked.

Mr. Fox scratched his chin. "It is impossible to say for certain, but I think it likely. It seems that anyone associated with this business is in jeopardy. You and I have been twice targeted for death and I think it safe to presume that either Colonel McCrea had information that would have helped us, or if our adversaries were not certain of that fact, they were at least willing to err on the side of caution and remove the possibility."

"This is unbelievable," Shelby muttered.

"Mr. Fox, sir. I have the things that you requested," a voice called from the door.

"Come in, lad," Fox called back. "Just lay them on the cot there. Thank you," he ended as the teen retreated from the tent.

Shelby shook off his bewilderment and saw that the soldier had delivered a set of woodsman's clothing and a pile of traps and snares used for capturing small game. Fox began to strip himself of his Quaker apparel and don the new garments.

Reading the captain's expression, Fox explained: "I may be entering the lion's den so I thought it prudent to assume the guise of a trapper for my trip to Fort Edward. One of the villains knows us by sight, but if there are others, they may only be relying on the same general description we found upon that one ambusher."

"You were going to tell me what you would like me to do; before Colonel Varick arrived to inform us about Colonel

McCrea," Shelby stated, wondering about his own facet of the mission.

"While I am away," Fox replied, pulling on a green hunting frock. "I need you to canvass the encampment for individuals who knew Miss McCrea. As tactfully as possible, inquire about her loyalties and character. Try to find out anything possible about the woman."

"Won't it seem odd, me asking questions about her? How will we keep our mission confidential?"

"Explain that you have been sent to make an official report," he replied, slipping on deerskin leggings. "That is a plausible explanation and will not reveal our true intention of uncovering which version of her death is the true one."

Mr. Fox exchanged his broad-brimmed black hat for a deerskin cap. He had begun to pack the traps into his saddle bags as he was speaking but halted and looked his partner in the eye. "Captain, this job I am giving you is an important one. You must appear to be collecting information for a routine report and please take accurate notes as you interview. However, you must not only record data but attune yourself to inflection of voice, facial expressions and body language as well. Your intuition will be a valuable asset. As you jot your notes, include not only what they tell you, but your own perceptions as well."

Shelby felt a sense of apprehension. "Mr. Fox, perhaps you should conduct these interviews yourself. I simply do not share your gifts of observation and inference."

"It is not possible for me to do it, Captain. I cannot be in two places at once. You will do fine. You may not be able to interpret what someone's inflection or expression suggests but you will know if it suggests *something*. When I return you will give me an account and I will know if I should follow up with an individual. Do you have any other questions?"

The explanation soothed Shelby's concern and he decided to use the opportunity to query the investigator on another subject.

"Actually I do, but it is along a different line. I noticed the inscription upon your magnifying lens. Do you actually know Dr. Franklin?" he asked, truly curious about Fox's association with the great man.

Mr. Fox's lips curled into that now familiar smirk. "You see, Captain, your powers of observation are more astute than you give yourself credit. Yes, I know him. I was born in Philadelphia and my grandfather was a friend of Ben Franklin. They were both members of a club called *The Junto.*" He turned back to his packing as he continued. "It was a mutual improvement society where the constituents debated and discussed morals, politics, and science. As a boy I was a frequent visitor to Dr. Franklin's home and he liked my inquisitive mind. I often assisted him in a variety of experiments and he made a gift of that magnifying lens to me on one such occasion."

Shelby listened in fascination. He had not really expected any substantial explanation from his secretive companion and was shocked not only that Fox truly was a personal acquaintance of the world-famous man but also that he had shed a sliver of light upon his past. The young soldier viewed this revelation with a bit of pride, sensing it a sign that he was gaining a trust the clandestine man shared with few people.

"One more thing, Captain. Be on your guard. As I said, we have already been targeted twice and our being together is what kept us alive. I would not have been able to handle those ruffians on the road alone. Had you not been with me, I would no longer be alive. And had I not awakened the other night, the assassin would have made short work of *you.* Now with us separated, we will be easier prey. Although I believe that the fellow has fled, he may return. He may even have been the one who disposed of Colonel McCrea; and that was just outside this very encampment. Be very careful, Captain," he warned. "Varick seems genuine enough..." he scratched his chin as if considering the colonel's legitimacy. "But if you absolutely need someone you can rely upon, seek out Josiah. He and I have worked together before. I would trust him with my life."

Mr. Fox's comments were disquieting to the young officer. Shelby had had some trepidation about his partner's departure, but it had only stemmed from his concern that he did not have the requisite experience to fulfill his assignment. He had not considered that their separation might increase the hazards to his personal safety.

Mr. Fox's lower legs had always looked the part of a woodsman, but now that visage extended upward to his whole frame. Gone was the Quaker gentleman and in his place stood a backwoods pioneer. Fox threw his bags over his shoulder and grabbed up his rifle. "I expect to see you in a few days," he said, shifting Shelby's focus from his uneasy reflection. "Don't wander off. Remain here at camp and uncover what you can about the unfortunate Miss McCrea," he said, extending his hand.

Shelby had become so used to saluting that the act of a handshake had taken him off guard. He smiled and warmly grasped the hand of the investigator, feeling that their bond had grown beyond that of a professional partnership. "You be careful too, Mr. Fox. I at least have Josiah to fall back upon but you will be on your own." Fox's crooked half-smile was the only reply before he vanished through the tent opening.

*   *   *

Mr. Fox warily led his horse northward. In order to add authenticity to his guise as a trapper, he also trailed a mule borrowed from the army's stock. Beasts of burden were never numerous enough for either army and the Patriots' willingness to loan one to Fox demonstrated the weight carried by the fact that he was on a mission for General Washington himself.

71

The American encampment at Stillwater was on the western bank of the Hudson whereas Fort Edward was situated upon the opposite shore. He would eventually have to ford the river, but it would be prudent to travel northward along the western side for as long as possible. Burgoyne was of course encamped at Fort Edward, but ten miles below that was another fort, Fort Miller, also in enemy hands. Undoubtedly there would be British patrols and pickets upon the western side as well, but the number of hostiles would be sparse as compared to the thick quantity milling about the land between the two forts.

The traveler had swung wide of the town of Saratoga which lay only three miles downriver from Fort Miller, albeit upon the opposite bank. Any Patriots in the vicinity had surely fled southward and he was concerned that the Tories who remained might attempt to conscript his animals. Beyond the town he drifted back eastward, again following the Hudson to where the stream known as "Batten Kill" spilled into the river upon the opposite bank.

The practiced woodsman concealed himself amongst the foliage and affixed his astute vision upon a curious site across the river. A column of what he estimated to be about eight-hundred men was moving south out of Fort Miller. He counted only a handful of red coats but there were more than three-hundred Hessians, easily identified by their blue coats and rigid, disciplined march. Each carried a heavy saber and wore cavalry riding boots indicating to Fox's practiced eye that they were dragoons; or mounted infantry. Unfortunately for these particular soldiers, they were on foot. No dragoon, Fox knew, walked unless he was without a mount. He thus surmised that this detachment must be embarking on a foraging expedition to forcibly seize horses from the locals. A sizable Loyalist militia force followed the Hessians and the presence of more than a hundred Indian warriors further confirmed the man's opinion that this army was bent on plunder. He shook his head in disgust as he imagined the savage thievery and destruction that undoubtedly lay ahead.

Fox continued to watch the column as it headed in a southeasterly direction, marching toward the Vermont border and the Green Mountains. The cunning investigator remained motionless until the entire force was out of sight. He was aware that John Stark, an old comrade of his from the last war, had been given an independent command in his native New Hampshire. After being passed over for promotion following the Battle of Trenton the fiery man had resigned from the Continental Army. He, like Schuyler, had been a casualty of the influence peddling so prevalent in the politics of war. He smiled when he thought of Stark. He knew that the old Indian fighter would be far more effective operating on his own rather than if he had received the coveted promotion and remained in the official chain of command. Stark had been Robert Rogers' second in command during the French and Indian conflict and his methods and abilities were far more suited to unconventional and improvisational maneuvers than following regimented orders from a traditionally-minded superior. Before leaving his place of concealment, Fox offered up a silent prayer that his old ally would be prepared for the inevitable encounter with this enemy detachment.

Within a few miles he had found a suitable place to ford the river and his horse ambled along the east bank of the Hudson as he approached Fort Edward. The traveler was wary; alert for any sign of trouble. He expected that if he encountered a British patrol, he may be detained and questioned. But that is not what most concerned him. His caution and heightened vigilance were mainly out of fear of Indian ambush. He knew that his horse and mule, weapons, and traps were prizes for the natives and that they would not hesitate to pounce on him for such booty, heedless of Burgoyne's order against such savagery.

Fox carefully scanned his surroundings but his inquisitiveness was more than mere prudence. It had been over fifteen years since he had last been in this country and he identified a variety of landmarks and places he had known during that melancholy and violent time. In those days Fort Edward had been a vital portage for troops travelling northward for Lake George or the head of Lake Champlain. He knew that all that remained of the old fort were ruins, but his mind's eye could easily envision the days spent living behind its then robust fortifications when it had been the base of operations of Rogers' Rangers.

Fox alertly tilted his head. He had heard an odd noise up ahead and he struggled to discern its origin. The sound was like a hollow, dull, thud. A moment later he heard it again. The road was tree-lined, and he scanned the neighboring forest. The noise did not alarm him. It was obviously the work of a single individual, but it intrigued him nonetheless. He had gone another fifty feet and the noise sounded again. Fox stopped in front of a row of fir trees off to the right of the roadway and then heard the sound once more. It came from somewhere behind the line of conifers. Fox spurred his horse around the artificial wall of trees to find a small meadow containing a dozen apple trees. To one side of the clearing sat the charred remains of a cabin.

Scanning one of the closest trees his curiosity was put to rest. There he found a dark haired boy, of perhaps nine or ten years perched among the branches. Below him was a barrel in which the lad had apparently been tossing down the fruit. The boy was frozen, obviously hoping he would avoid detection. The look on his face spelled alarm.

"Hello there, son."

"Umm. Howdy mister," he replied, nervously glancing at the barrel as if it were treasure and Fox a pirate.

"It's lucky that those apples escaped Burgoyne's scouts."

74

"They've been up and down the road, but they didn't think to look behind the trees."

"Is this your orchard?"

The boy gulped. "Kind of. This land belonged to my grandfather but in the last war, the Huron burned him out," he replied, nodding toward the cabin's remains. "Our house is in Fort Edward but we still claim title to this land," he stated, again shooting an apprehensive glance at the barrel.

"Don't worry, son," Fox laughed in the silent manner of his. "I regard those apples as your property. I won't take them from you. If you'd consent though, I'd like to buy one. How's a shilling?"

"Really? You won't take them?" His distraught expression melted into a smile. "Sure, mister a shilling would be great."

Fox nudged his horse forward and handed the boy up the silver.

"Here you are, fresh off of the tree," the lad replied, exchanging an apple for the coin.

Fox took the fruit and added, "You know, I haven't been this way for a long time, but I have kin in the area. Can you tell me where I can find Miss Jane McCrea?"

The boy's smile faded. "Gee mister I'm sorry to tell you, but Miss McCrea is dead. The Indians got her about two weeks ago."

Fox feigned shock. He sighed heavily and shook his head in dismay. "Do you know where she's buried? I would like to pay my respects."

"Yes, sir. Her fiancé, Lieutenant Jones, had her buried. If you follow the road you'll see a small cemetery off to the left about three miles shy of the village."

"How about her brother? I know he lives around here. Can you direct me to his home?"

"Well sir, his cabin is about a mile beyond the cemetery, but he's not there. He's a rebel you know, so he fled when the

75

lobsterbacks moved into Fort Edward. But if I was you, I'd steer clear of that house. Some Hessians moved in there and the way I hear it, they're as bad as the Indians. Some say they eat the hearts of those they kill in battle."

"Hmm. Well I guess I'll just have to catch up with Cousin John some other time, then. Did you know Jane?" he asked, in an attempt to bleed some information about his alleged relative.

"Sure," he said somewhat somberly, as if reflecting on the fact that she was no longer of this world.

"Why did the Indians turn on her? She was a Tory wasn't she?" he questioned, trying to ascertain her loyalties.

"She was to marry Lieutenant Jones and he's a Tory but I don't know if she was. She hadn't lived here all that long. I suppose the Indians killed her for her hair. They go crazy for a good scalp and she had a fine head of hair. Whatever the reason, people around hereabouts are scared straight. Them that wasn't rebels before are joining up with the militias to fight the Redcoats. They know if the Redcoats go, so do the Indians."

Fox rubbed the fruit on his shirt and took a bite. Thank you kindly for the apple," he said as he chewed. "Oh, and son I won't tell anyone about your little orchard if you promise not to tell anyone about me. I'm just a simple trapper and I don't want any trouble."

"Yes, sir. I won't say anything. And thanks for the shilling."

The little graveyard was easy to find. A picket fence along the roadside encircled the area where faded white headstones from the last century sat alongside markers for the more recently entombed. The McCrea woman's grave was readily apparent by the still unsettled earth in front of the simple wooden placard that announced the girl's resting place. Fox bowed his head and silently prayed for the murder victim. After he had finished his invocation, he surveyed his surroundings and mentally recorded

76

the location before climbing back aboard his horse and moving off in the direction of Fort Edward.

With some difficulty he ascended a heavily wooded hill east of the old fort. Once atop the knoll he climbed a towering oak and looked down upon his former haunt. The forest around the neglected stronghold had been cleared for a couple of miles and farmhouses and fields of grain occupied what had once been woodlands. He could see the enemy encampment where the British and their dreaded Hessian collaborators sat, languidly awaiting supplies and artillery from Ticonderoga. If Burgoyne had been alarmed by the news that Howe would not be striking out from the city he was making no show of it. The general was known to be both a *play*wright and a *play*boy and Fox wondered if his lack of haste was an affectation of dramatic flair or the habitual laziness of a libertine.

Fox remained high atop the tree, making himself comfortable in the crook of a stout branch. He sat patiently in his perch upon the hillside, waiting for darkness to fall. His animals had been tethered securely to sturdy trees and enough wild blueberry bushes were within their range that they would be contented for some time to come. The faux trapper continued to watch the movements in the camp below as he silently ate a cold meal of salted pork retrieved from his pouch. Despite his education and civil manners he was long practiced in such bucolic living. Some might have found the duration maddening, but the quasi-Quaker had long ago learned the value of noiseless patience. In fact it often could mean the difference between life and death on the American frontier. And of course he had a book full of Greeks and Trojans to keep him company during his treetop vigil.

Eventually the pink horizon faded into velvety blackness and campfires began to twinkle to life below. A few large purplish clouds crawled slowly overhead as a pale, full moon peaked over the horizon. One by one the glimmer of a thousand pinpricks of light began to pierce the night sky. Silently he descended from his lookout.

The watcher took a last gulp from his canteen and slung a carefully packed haversack over his shoulders. He slid the tomahawk into its familiar spot at the small of his back and felt for the handle of his knife, making sure it was snug in its sheath. Gripping his rifle around the stock, he quietly then he crept down the hillside, his deerskin moccasins emitting only the faintest whisper.

Chapter 8

His destination would be most simply achieved by retracing his way down the hillside and following the road that led south from Fort Edward. Burgoyne's men had cleared most of the trees felled under orders of the retreating General Schuyler, at least within the vicinity of the village. However, the investigator resolved to avoid contact with anyone if possible. Certainly enemy patrols and Indian scouting parties were of concern, but so were civilians. Noncombatants were always in and out of the British camps and although those who had no love for the British often related intelligence to the Patriots, others brought information *to* the King's men. Even though he was operating in disguise he did not welcome any unnecessary encounters. He believed, or at least hoped, that the boy in the orchard would not discuss his presence. But even if he did, it was more likely that one would dismiss the encounter as exactly what Fox had presented it as: a trapper out plying his trade. A run-in at night however was much more likely to arouse suspicion and possibly invite an attack upon his person. Contact with any of the aforementioned may occur, but he would not invite it. No, he would avoid the road this night. So upon reaching the base of the hill Fox moved off through the woods, his uncanny eyesight almost cat-like under the dim canopy of the nighttime forest.

Two hours had passed and the moon had climbed further overhead. It reflected a moderate degree of light, but the patches of large, puffy cumulus clouds that sluggishly plodded across the sky frequently obscured the milky orb. Fox remained hidden behind the trunk of a large pine, silently scanning the roadway with not only his eyes, but his ears as well. Only after ten minutes of observation did he quietly skulk across the path and push open the picket gate of the cemetery.

For some reason the chirping of the nighttime insects seemed more subdued in this forlorn setting and as if to accentuate the sullen atmosphere, an owl croaked morosely from somewhere in the gloom.

Fox had spent too many nights in the forest and too much time in the company of fallen warriors to be distracted by the ghoulish ambiance, and moved directly to his task. He knelt before the wooden headstone and unslung the bag from his back. He then removed the small entrenching shovel he had procured from the Stillwater encampment. Pulling the tomahawk from his back, Fox laid it next to his pack and rifle, making sure that it was within reach should a need arise. He then took the shovel and began chopping into the earth. His chore was a grisly one, but its macabre nature made no impression upon him; unearthing the unfortunate girl was necessary.

Even though his military service had been almost exclusively spent in the wilds of the frontier, Fox was no stranger to the mechanics of building defenses. He had endured many an hour digging foxholes and trenches as well as piling soil in the construction of redoubts and breastworks. Thus it took neither great effort nor time before his spade had displaced the loose earth of the recent grave and found the solid barrier of the pine lid.

Despite the relative ease with which he had uncovered the coffin, Mr. Fox had dug prudently and patiently, often halting and listening to make sure no traveler on the roadway might happen upon him. He now did the same, but for a longer duration, before producing his tinder box. The full moon at this point was high in the heavens and the clouds had mercifully parted, but he would still need the aid of a candle to minutely inspect the corpse. With a flash of flint upon steel the small

80

piece of charcloth ignited. He dipped the candle's wick into the tiny blaze before it petered out.

Carefully, he set the candle in the mound of overturned earth that now rimmed the oblong hole he had created. A series of soft hisses sounded as he brushed the remaining dirt from the top of the casket. Fox withdrew his knife from its sheath and slid the blade under the lid. Without much effort the covering came loose. Before removing the top, the patient man again sat in silence, straining to hear any hint of movement upon the nearby road. Once satisfied, he pulled the plank off and gently placed it next to the open grave. The stench of death was not new to him, yet he had to steady himself to dismiss the reek of decomposition.

He reached for the candle and brought it down over the head of the ill-fated girl. The sight of a scalping victim was truly a grotesque visage, and sadly, the pious man had bore witness to the aftermath of the atrocity more times than he could count. Fox was stoic by both nature and practice but the spectacle of a scalped person always unleashed a visceral hatred born from the adolescent tragedy that had changed his path in life.

Aside from the hideous sight of the exposed skull where the scalp had been cut away, two other wounds were visible. First, Mr. Fox examined the vicious cleave wrought through the upper section of the girl's forehead. The telltale mark of the tomahawk was unmistakable. The second injury was on the side of the head where a bullet hole cut through the straggled and bloody remnants of what had obviously once been comely and lush fields of blond hair.

The investigator reached into his bag and removed his glasses-case and placed his spectacles in that familiar spot on the end of his nose. He lowered the candle within inches of the opening the musket ball had forged. Fox scratched his chin pensively. He replaced his eyeglasses in their case and again plunged his hand into the haversack, retrieving the gift from the

81

eminent Dr. Franklin. With candle in one hand and magnifying glass in the other, Fox carefully scrutinized the gunshot wound. He put the candle between his teeth and touched at the area that darkened the flaxen tresses near the puncture. After a soft grunt of displeasure he extinguished the candle and pulled himself from the grave. He sat silently upon its brim, listening once more for even the faintest tread upon the road. Content that he was still alone, he replaced the lid upon the pine box and began to re-cover the ill-fated bride-to-be.

Before departing, the Quaker again spent a solemn moment in prayer before the marker. He then slipped away, leaving the occupants of that somber place to resume their eternal rest.

It was past midnight, but the investigator's undertaking was but half accomplished. Rather than return to his hillside camp, he stealthily made his way toward the home of Colonel John McCrea.

He crouched and slowly pulled aside a low-hanging spruce bough. Some fifty yards ahead he could make out the faint outline of a squat, darkened structure. An overgrown garden occupied the distance between his position and that of the house. He cast his vision upon the chimney-top and the absence of smoke was a welcome sign. No light appeared in either of the two windows that faced him. Fox slowly stood, hiding behind the branches. He angled his head this way and that, spying for any hint of dim candlelight that might have been unobservable from his crouched position. A man of Mr. Fox's experience could never fully gratify his trepidation but he was convinced enough to advance. He waited patiently as a cloud crept in front of the moon. Little by little it ate away at the pallid sphere and a shadow inched over the open space between the sleuth and the cabin. As soon as the interval was eclipsed he vacated his post and quickly, silently, and invisibly skirted the clearing before melting into the murk at the side of the house.

Slowly, he edged his way along the side of the cabin until he reached a window. Carefully, he peeked an eye past the pane. The faint glow of embers smoldered in the fireplace across the room. Obviously, the remains of the fire were not potent enough to produce visible smoke atop the chimney, but the pale cinders were in all likelihood the remnants of a cooking fire and indicated that the house was certainly occupied. Visually, he began to search the room and observed four curious lumps upon the floor. The light was insufficient for any detailed study, but experience and common sense indicated that the mounds were soldiers stretched out upon their bedrolls.

Furtively, Fox then moved around the house peering into its other windows. The cabin was a simple one; a mere three rooms. Aside from the parlor where the fireplace was located, there was a small pantry and bedroom. In the bedroom a single bed contained two more shapeless forms. Having obtained as much intelligence as he thought possible, the counterfeit trapper slipped away from the cabin and dissolved back into the forest.

In the woods Fox found the large trunk of a toppled willow tree a few thousand yards from the McCrea house. Using his entrenching shovel and tomahawk Mr. Fox dug out a hollow alongside. He lined the bottom with spruce branches and then expertly camouflaged the recess with a variety of skillfully interlaced branches. The trained woodsman lifted the woven blind and slid into the cavity. In minutes he was under his special brand of half-sleep that had so marveled Captain Shelby.

Early the next day Fox crept through the forest and found an advantageous vantage point from which to spy on the McCrea house. Smoke now wafted from the chimney as the German soldiers were apparently preparing their morning meal. He could make out shapes moving past the windows and even heard an occasional exclamation or burst of laughter.

He had hoped to have a look around the interior of the home before gathering his animals and departing for Stillwater but he now thought that this might not be possible. He had neither the rations nor time to linger very long and if the mercenaries lodging within the cabin were in no hurry to vacate, he would simply have to forgo the inspection and journey back to the American lines to see what, if anything, Captain Shelby had uncovered.

Fox looked apprehensively at the darkening sky. Rain was on the way and he measured his desire to explore the home with his hope to get underway before the clouds opened up. The watcher held out for an hour but at the end of that duration he resigned that he must leave. He turned to begin picking his way carefully back to his hillside camp but just as he did so, the unmistakable tattoo of hurried hoof beats reverberated through the air. The sound grew louder and within thirty seconds a rider appeared. A junior officer clad in the telltale blue of the Hessian military pulled up in front of the cabin and called out something in the harsh and biting tones of the German language as he vaulted from the saddle. A moment later the half dozen occupants of the house emerged onto the front porch and an animated conversation commenced. The exchange lasted less than a minute before the messenger was again atop his mount and galloping back down the road toward the encampment at Fort Edward.

The unwelcome tenants scurried back inside and a great commotion could be heard within. The discipline and efficiency of the Hessian troops was evident even in the chaos of this surprise summons as it was only a matter of minutes before they emerged again, dressed and outfitted for duty. Each was not only carrying a short heavy bore German rifle, but their haversacks, cartridge boxes, and canteens as well. It was obvious that a march had been ordered and these men were being called to immediately join the ranks at Fort Edward.

Fox waited patiently for the soldiers to disappear down the dusty road before he cautiously approached the cabin. He peered down the thoroughfare to make sure the mercenaries had gone and then climbed onto the porch and pressed an ear to the home's door. Once content that the abode was empty, he pushed open the portal. Despite the haste of the departure the interior was in surprisingly neat appearance. The uninvited residents had preformed no debauchery or vandalism to the place and the only evidence of their stay was the smoldering logs in the fireplace, the faint aroma of cooked sausages, and a forgotten bayonet that had been left upon the table.

It had not really been necessary for Fox to examine the house, but he was a thorough man and once an enigma presented itself he was stubborn about letting go until he had every piece of a puzzle in place. There may be nothing of value to be learned here, especially given that any evidence of the McCrea's lives may have been swept away by the more recent occupants but since the opportunity had provided itself, the investigator could not resist poking around.

The parlor held some simple furniture; a few chairs, a cupboard, and a table. Fireplace tools rested in their wrought-iron stand next to a pair of humbly designed andirons. Above the mantel widely spaced pegs denoted the spot where Colonel McCrea's rifle once hung. Thoughtlessly, Fox played with the handle of the fireplace poker as he looked around the room, lost in thought. Before long, he moved into the bedroom, mindlessly carrying the poker with him as a sort of make-shift walking stick.

The bed chamber was as modestly rustic as the rest of the house. A trunk, possibly once a sea-chest, sat at the foot of the bed but an exploration of the box revealed nothing more than a few articles of clothing and a knitted blanket. He thoughtlessly tapped the poker on the wide-planked floor as he shifted to the simple pantry at the rear of the house. A small work table stood against the wall and a wooden basin rested upon its surface. He picked through a side-board where some plates and mugs were kept as well as some spices and other cooking implements and utensils. Some items appeared to be missing, but whether they had been commandeered by the Hessians or taken by the retreating Miss McCrea, he could only guess.

With nothing else to see, Mr. Fox came back into the main room and headed for the door before noticing that he still held the poker in his hand. His lips curled into his characteristic half-smile as he smirked at his forgetfulness and crossed to the hearth to replace the tool in its holder. As he leaned the handle against the iron of the stand, it slipped and fell over, its handle striking the wooden floor with a curiously hollow thud.

Fox's brows wrinkled inquisitively. He leaned his rifle in the nearby corner and tapped a forefinger upon his chin as he looked down at a small hole in the floorboard. It appeared to be no more than the space left by a dislodged knot. He knelt down for a closer look and moved the poker to one side of the plank and fitted his finger into the opening. Hooking his finger on the underside of the board, he pulled upward and the plank lifted out of place.

Peering into the recessed area, he could see that it contained a small, lidded wooden box about eight inches in length and four inches in both height and width. He reached down into the crevice and lifted out the container. The top came off easily. Inside he found a number of vials. One by one he held them up to the light. Each contained a clear liquid but some were marked with the letter "A" others a "B" and a third with a "C". He gripped one designated as "A" firmly in his left hand and twisted at the cork stopper with his right. With a slight "pop" the plug came loose. Cautiously, he brought his nose near the lip of the vial.

"Cobalt chloride," he whispered to himself.

Replacing the cork he applied the same test to a bottle marked with a "B" and indentified the aroma as that of glycerine. By now he was certain what the third bottle contained, but for good measure he tried that one as well and detected the scent

86

produced when the contents of each of the other chemicals was mixed together. He had just set the vial back into the box when an alarming sound reached his ear. The thud of a heavy footstep echoed from the front porch. With lightning speed he shoved the box into the hole and slid the floorboard back in place, although it missed the mark precisely and sat tilted in the aperture. Grabbing the fireplace poker that he had left next to the opening, he leapt backward, throwing himself against the wall adjacent to the front door, so that he would be hidden from view as the person entered.

The door flung open and a Hessian grenadier burst into the room. He hurried directly over to the table, grumbling unintelligibly under his breath in German. The man was a virtual giant, at least six and a half feet in height but appeared even taller as his high mitered hat came within inches of the ceiling. The soldier's back was to Fox and the intrepid investigator pulled the swinging door further open so as to hide himself once the intruder turned around. The soldier muttered some Germanic statement of relief as he reclaimed his forgotten bayonet. Fox could see him through the slats that made up the simple door. He shoved the weapon into his belt and made an about face toward the doorway. Fox narrowed his eyes, ready for action should the mercenary detect his presence. Fortunately, the man was so hurried that he stomped directly through the passageway, grabbing hold of the handle as he passed, closing the door behind him.

Fox breathed a sigh of relief. However a mere moment later the door flung open again, smashing the Patriot up against the wall. Despite the Hessian's haste to retrieve his bayonet, his peripheral vision had registered either the misplaced floorboard or the rifle leaning in the corner, but the image had not registered upon his distracted mind until he was on the porch. Hastily he had returned to determine the cause.

The door had slammed Fox's head into the hard horizontal logs that made up the cabin's walls, rendering him momentarily senseless. The soldier had felt the resistance met by the door and instantly knew where the man had been hiding. He was too close, and it would have been too time-consuming, for him to have moved back and unslung his rifle so he pulled the bayonet from his belt, and with an angry cry leapt toward his stunned opponent.

With a reaction that was near instinct, Mr. Fox deflected the man's weapon with the fireplace poker he still held in his hand. The Hessian possessed unbelievable strength. The bayonet buried itself an inch deep in the log wall. Fox reacted immediately. Driving his shoulder into the man's ribs, he shoved him backward across the room with all of his might, the bayonet left protruding from the wall. The pair toppled over the table and slammed violently upon the opposite wall, landing in a heap upon the floor. The two men struggled ferociously upon the ground in the small space between the toppled table and wall. Despite Fox's skill the huge Hessian succeeded in getting on top, pinning the Patriot down. He began to rein blows down upon Fox's face with his huge mitt-like fists. Fox had lost the poker when they had gone over the table, his tomahawk was trapped behind his back, and his knife was pinned under the German who sat upon his midsection.

Desperately, Fox grabbed at the man's face and for his neck between deflecting the punishing blows. He felt the barrel of the man's rifle, still slung behind his back and in sheer desperation clawed at it. Unbelievable good fortune shined upon him as the end of the rifle strap tore loose and the gun clattered to the floor next to them. It was within easy reach of the pinned man and sudden fear froze on the Hessian's face as he rolled off of his opponent desperate to reclaim the gun before it could be used against him.

As the German knelt to pick up his weapon, Fox jumped upon his back, reaching past him to grab the strap that was still affixed to the butt-end of the rifle. He pulled it tight around his foe's neck and squeezed with all of his might. The huge Hessian clutched at his throat, trying franticly to pull the leather band away from his windpipe. He stood; the tenacious investigator still upon his back. As Mr. Fox hung on for dear life, the giant began thrashing around the room, smashing him into the walls, the heavy rifle clattering on the floor as it was dragged around the room by the pair of combatants. The Hessian's face had begun to discolor and his eyes popped from their sockets. Finally he fell to his knees, and five seconds later, flat upon his face.

The sweaty and exhausted Patriot waited a precautionary full minute before he slackened his grip upon the enemy's neck. Finally he rolled off of him and stretched his cramped fingers. Gingerly, he touched at his bruised cheek. He sat up and looked around at the shambles. The room was almost unrecognizable from the neat interior that had existed just minutes before.

Fox pulled loose his tomahawk and knife and crawled over to the dead man. The best practice now, he knew, was to brain the man and scalp him. That way when his comrades found him they would conclude that Indians had fallen upon him when he returned to the McCrea house. This would not only be a logical blind to his true fate, but would also further the notion of Indian savagery and probably even have the valuable effect of brewing hostilities within Burgoyne's ranks between his Indian scouts and Hessian troops.

He raised the tomahawk above his head and clenched his teeth. Suddenly his arm slackened and he dropped it without striking the blow. Despite Fox's experience as an Indian fighter, despite his willingness to overlook certain principles for a greater objective, he could not bring himself to do it. It was the best tactic. He knew it. However, the practice of scalping, and

89

the scar it had left upon him was so indelible, that he abandoned the plan and replaced his weapons. Instead, he hefted the huge body over his shoulder and carried it to the place where he had slept the night before. He rolled the man into the hollowed out space under the log and hurried back to the cabin and quickly straightened it up. He removed the box of chemicals, which he had resolved to take with him, and then replaced the ill-fitting floorboard, leaving the hiding place completely vacant. He collected not only his own rifle, but the soldier's rifle and hat and scurried back to the burial place, shoving both items in with their owner. The woven screen was put in place and as was his practice, Mr. Fox said a quiet prayer for the soul of the deceased.

Balancing stealth with haste, Fox made a bee-line for his hillside encampment. The Hessians had left the McCrea place speedily and whatever task had called them away might be pressing enough that they would not immediately be able to investigate the absence of their friend. However, to be safe he wanted to quickly put as much space between the cabin and himself as possible. As he climbed the wooded knoll, he hoped that his camp had not been discovered. Not only might he have another fight on his hands, but even if locals or Indians had merely stolen his goods and animals, he did not look forward to walking back to Stillwater. Fortunately his horse and mule were still there, munching contentedly upon the blueberries.

It took him no more than a few minutes to collect his things and pack them upon the animals. A rain had begun to fall, but before departing he decided to ascend the tree once more to survey the British encampment. Any information he might ascertain about the number and disposition of the enemy might be helpful to the commander back at Stillwater.

Once atop the tree, he spied scores of red coats milling about the tents but he also perceived what had drawn the Hessians away from the cabin. A column of some six-hundred of the German mercenaries was marching southward. Fox counted a company of riflemen, a battalion of light infantry and grenadiers, and two six-pound cannon. This deployment brought the half-smile to Mr. Fox's lips. These were reinforcements; apparently his old comrade John Stark *had* been ready for the Hessians he had seen headed for Vermont.

Chapter 9

Captain Shelby was startled from his sleep by a great commotion outside. He recognized the clamor as it was one he had heard many times. The camp was being broken up. Alertness washed over him as he pushed himself from his cot and quickly dressed. Emerging into the sunlight, his ears were vindicated by the sight of tents being disassembled as wagons and men scurried about.

"Colonel Varick! Colonel Varick!" he called, seeing the officer some distance off giving instructions to a group of men loading a wagon. Shelby started toward the colonel, but Varick finished with the teamsters and met the captain halfway.

"Colonel Varick, is Burgoyne advancing?" he surmised at the reason for breaking the camp, ready to lend any aid he could in the face of such an emergency.

"No, Captain," Varick returned in a reassuring tone. "But as you know the relief column left for Fort Stanwix yesterday and with their departure the British have a decided numeric advantage. There is no evidence that Burgoyne is on the move but just to be safe General Schuyler has decided to fall back to the Sprouts."

"The Sprouts?"

"Oh, I'm sorry," the colonel apologized, recalling that Shelby was not native to the area. "The Sprouts are a series of islands where the Mohawk empties into the Hudson. It is only a short distance from here but a much more defensible position."

"Captain," Varick continued, "I have a team of men querying the various units to find any who knew the McCrea woman. I will let you know when I have collected them."

Shelby marveled at Varick's efficiency. "Colonel, I am sure that you have your hands full with this withdrawal. I can certainly wait until the camp is reassembled at 'the Sprouts.'"

Varick waved off the notion. "That is very kind of you Captain, but I set the search in motion before the general issued the order to decamp. Although it is a bit chaotic, I think we'll be able to accomplish both operations at the same time. If you wouldn't mind, I suggest that you pack your things and those of Mr. Fox as well. Within the hour some men will be by to strike your tent."

Captain Shelby did just as the colonel had suggested, and even had time to wash, shave, and grab a bite before the team arrived to collapse his tent. He made sure that their possessions were accounted for and accessible under the supervision of a reliable private provided by the colonel. Shelby could not sit idly by while he waited for Varick's summons and began hefting tents and equipment into wagons alongside common laborers and enlisted men. It was just this lack of pretension that had endeared him to the Marylanders under his command during the battles in New York and New Jersey.

A harried corporal appeared where Shelby and Fox's tent had once been. He stood looking around searchingly. Finally his eyes fell upon the industrious captain laboring a short distance away.

"Captain Shelby?" he asked, rushing over.

"Yes," he replied, returning the man's salute.

"Begging your pardon, sir but Colonel Varick sent me for you. He said to tell you that the people you requested are assembled. He found a tent that is still standing in case you wanted to use it for your interviews."

"That sounds perfect," Shelby replied, dusting off his hands. "Which way?"

"About a quarter mile in that direction sir," he said, pointing. "I believe it's the only tent left up so it should be easy to find."

"Thank you, Corporal." The pair exchanged salutes again and Shelby patted his pocket to ensure that he had both notebook and pencil before heading off to meet with the acquaintances of the ill-fated Jane McCrea.

Shelby negotiated marching companies, hustling wagons, ox drawn artillery pieces and dozens of other obstacles in the short distance to the lone tent. There he found almost a dozen people waiting for him. Five were militiamen, leaning on their rifles chatting affably. Another three were local men who were being employed as teamsters and seemed irritated to be dragged away from their wagons. A boy about the age of twelve, was also there. He sat cross-legged on the ground tapping on a drum, practicing a variety of cadences. There were also two women with the group. One was the wife of one of the militiamen and the other was a camp follower who had been eking out a living as a washerwoman for whatever soldiers might despise filthy clothing more than parting with some silver.

"Hello," he announced his presence to the group. "I am Captain Shelby." All turned their attention to the officer. "I have been sent up from General Washington's command to compile a report on the murder of Miss Jane McCrea. I apologize for taking your time. This is all really just a routine inquiry and I will be through shortly. Since the camp is being broken down, why don't I begin with you men," he said to the teamsters, "so that you can get back to work. I'd like to speak with you one at a time," he said, pulling back the tent flap as a tall, thin wagon master stepped forward.

Inside the tent were two upright logs functioning as stools and a larger third one between the two, which posed as a table. These rustic furnishing made the simple equipment of his own tent look lavish but he of course was grateful even for the luxury of a tent to use in the mayhem of an army's breaking camp.

Shelby pulled out his small notebook and readied his pencil. Unfortunately the driver had little to offer. He lived in Fort

Edward, and had known John McCrea for some time, but had only been in the deceased girl's company on a couple of occasions. He explained that she had come up from New Jersey to live with her brother and had not resided in the area for very long before her unfortunate demise. His interaction with her had been only short, polite conversation and he knew nothing of her political feelings nor could he offer any hypothesis as to why the Indians might kill her beyond their general penchant for savagery. The two other wagoners were no more helpful, echoing basically the same story as their slender compatriot.

Next Shelby interviewed the militiamen in turn and found that although all knew John McCrea, four of them only knew his sister in the most superficial of ways and did not provide the captain with any worthwhile information. The fifth was the man whose wife was also present. He had been a dear friend of John and he and his wife had dined at the McCrea house a number of times and found the girl to be quite talkative in their company. Shelby asked him to retrieve his wife so that he might speak with them together. The captain vacated his seat for the lady and rolled the center log out of its position as a table, using it as a stool for himself.

"Mrs. Jacobs," Shelby said to the thin, attractive woman in her mid-twenties. "Your husband tells me that you were both friendly with Miss McCrea."

"Yes, I suppose you could say so. She had only been living with John for a couple of months mind you but I recon that Otto and I," she motioned toward her husband, "probably knew her better than anyone else in the area; excepting her brother of course."

"I am trying to figure out why General Burgoyne's Indians murdered her. It doesn't seem logical for them to kill a Tory, especially if Lieutenant Jones had sent them to retrieve her."

"I don't know why they did it, other than it being in their basic nature to go after a scalp when it presents itself," Otto

95

Jacobs broke in. "But I don't know that she was a Tory. She didn't express ideas either for or against the Revolution, at least not around us." He looked to his wife for confirmation and she nodded her agreement with the assessment.

"I suppose then her affiliation with Lieutenant Jones was purely romantic. Did she ever speak of him?"

"Oh yes," Mrs. Jacobs returned. "Their families had been neighbors in New Jersey. They had grown up together. However their romance did not blossom until she moved up here. When he saw Jane again he was smitten! He pursued her with some vigor," she laughed as if recalling the man's efforts to woo the girl.

"How did Colonel McCrea feel about his sister being betrothed to a Loyalist?" the captain asked, scratching some details in his notebook. The couple looked at each other questioningly, and sensing their apprehension Shelby looked up from his writing. "Was he angry about that?"

Otto answered. "He seemed... uneasy about the situation. He... He didn't think much of David Jones."

"I should say not, as he was fighting for the opposing army," Shelby returned off-handedly as he returned to his pad but his pencil hesitated yet again as the woman offered further comment.

"I suppose..." Mrs. Jacobs mused. "He thought that his sister was making a mistake attaching herself to him. I tried to tell him that a woman's heart is governed by invisible forces and that whether he understood the attraction or not mattered little to a girl in love."

Shelby spent a few more minutes with the couple and then dismissed them, thanking them for their help. He next met with the drummer boy who was so fixated on proper performance of his beats that the captain had to snatch the sticks away in order to get his full attention. When Shelby asked about the character of the woman in question, the most he could pull out of the boy was that Jane McCrea was a "nice lady." He had assumed that the lad would have little to offer and was about to release him when the boy came through with a revelation.

"Like I said, I didn't know her much... But I saw the Indians take her."

"What? You saw them take her?"

"Uh huh," he nodded. "I was on the road heading south to join the militia. I was just about to pass the McNeil house when I saw the Indians coming. I jumped into a thicket across the road."

"Well what exactly did you see?" Shelby impatiently inquired.

"There were six of them. They were all in war-paint but the leader had his head, shoulders and chest covered in black and a white lightning bolt drawn across his face like this." He indicated a diagonal trajectory with his finger across his own face. "They kept calling him *Le Loup*."

"The wolf," Shelby muttered the French translation as he scribbled in his pad. "Go on."

"Well, both Miss McCrea and Mrs. McNeil came out and left with the Indians. That's it."

"Did the Indians treat them roughly?"

"No, it looked like they were friends."

"So you would say that the women left of their own accord?"

"Oh yes."

The boy had nothing more to offer, but Shelby was satisfied that he had provided at least *some* corroborative data. He thanked the lad and sent him on his way.

Finally the captain conducted his last interview, that with the washerwoman. The lady, a widow named Mrs. Braithwaite, was an overweight woman in her late thirties but the wears of life made her look much older. Her face was creased, and her dark brown hair streaked with gray.

97

"It's about time," she quipped acerbically. "I have things to do, you know."

"I'm sorry for the delay madam; I will attempt to be as brief as possible. How well did you know Miss McCrea?"

"Oh, I talked with her a few times. She was a Presbyterian, you know. Don't have a lot of time for Presbyterians."

"Some have said that our own militia shot her accidentally and I've been sent here to find out if that's true."

"What?" she squawked. "Ridiculous! The Indians got her. The militia pulled out before the Indians even took her."

"Yes, that is what I've been told," he replied, jotting some notes down. "She must have really loved Lieutenant Jones to linger rather than leaving with her brother and the militia," Shelby said, expressing his thoughts aloud as he wrote.

"I don't know about *that*," she cracked sarcastically.

Shelby's pencil stopped. "Oh?"

"I saw her sneaking around after dark with another man." The woman almost smiled, as if she enjoyed being the purveyor of gossip.

"Really?" The news shocked the interviewer and he wondered if the crone was inventing the tale. "Who was he?"

"That I can't say," the woman pouted in obvious disappointment. "But twice I saw her on the military road after sundown near the big oak. That's what we call a particular tree; 'the big oak,'" she explained. "They were in the shadows but I could tell that it was Jane. All I can tell you about the man is that he is an older chap."

"Older? If you couldn't see him clearly how do you know his age?"

"Because he is stooped."

"Stooped?"

"You know, bent over at the shoulders." She stood and demonstrated, leaning forward about twenty degrees. "I never saw a young man, crooked like that," she quipped.

Shelby's pencil went to work again. He rubbed his chin wondering if these liaisons had actually taken place and if so, if it had any bearing on the girl's death.

"Do you know Lieutenant Jones?" he asked as he scribbled.

"Certainly."

"And you're sure it wasn't him she was meeting? He may have slipped away from his command to meet with her."

She sniffed, offended by the assertion. "Of course it wasn't David. David's spine is as straight as an arrow."

"Perhaps he wore a disguise so as to avoid being captured by the militia?"

The woman scoffed again. "Even though this fellow was bent over, I can estimate his height at six feet. David is no more than five foot six."

The captain tapped the pencil on his lips and pondered, "An older man?"

Mrs. Braithwaite blurted, "Why not? My own departed husband was thirty years my senior!" Shelby could not tell if the resentment in her voice resulted from his questioning her recollection of the man, or if she thought that he was passing judgment on May-December romances.

"And when exactly was it that you witnessed these meetings?" the captain asked.

"Hmm," scratched her head. "The first time was early, maybe mid-spring. The second time was about a week before the girl was killed," she said with a conviction that dissuaded the officer from asking if she was sure.

Nothing more could be ascertained from Mrs. Braithwaite, so Shelby dismissed the camp-follower. He was intrigued by the information but also glad when the interview concluded, happy to be rid of the disagreeable woman. He puzzled over her story. Mrs. Jacobs, who seemed to know Jane McCrea well, was certain that she truly loved David Jones. Yet, Mrs. Braithwaite's account seemed to prove otherwise. He paged through his

99

booklet, double checking to be sure he had recorded every bit of information. He was uncertain if any of it would be of use to Mr. Fox, but he was at least content that he had fulfilled the job the investigator had assigned him.

Captain Shelby stepped from the tent, depositing his notebook into his breast pocket. He looked around questioningly, wondering where he might find Colonel Varick to inform him that he was finished and that the tent could be removed.

"William?" An oddly familiar voice called from behind him.

The captain turned to find a mounted man also bearing the rank of captain. "Rawlings? Is that you?" Shelby asked, his lips widening into a smile.

The man climbed down from his horse and embraced the captain warmly. "What are you doing here?" he asked Shelby through his grin.

"I've been sent up by General Alexander, well actually on orders from General Washington to report on the death of the McCrea girl. What about you? Last I saw you was White Plains."

"Yes. From there I was sent fifteen miles north to the Highlands in order to bolster Fort Montgomery. When it became clear that Howe was not coming north, I was detached to help out here against Burgoyne."

"Where are you going now? General Schuyler is withdrawing south but you were about to head out on the westerly road, if I'm not mistaken."

The grin melted from Rawlings' face. "That I was! Theodore Vanderslyke is among those trapped at Fort Stanwix. It took me this long to convince my superior to detach me for the expedition. He told me that I could only catch up with them if I was mounted, and that if I could get a horse he would allow me to go. I suspect that he never believed that I would be able to procure one," he said mockingly. "You don't even want to know what I had to pay for it! That bloody farmer robbed me," he grumbled through clenched teeth. "I'm heading out now to catch up with the relief force."

"Vanderslyke?" Shelby repeated the name. Both Captain Rawlings and Lieutenant Vanderslyke had fought with Shelby in the battles at Long Island, Brooklyn, and Manhattan. The trio had been close friends in those days and had saved one another's lives on more than one occasion.

Shelby considered Mr. Fox's warning to stay within the camp until his return, but quickly dismissed the command. "I've completed the task he left for me," he thought to himself. "I've nothing left to do here, and I've no idea when he'll return." He turned to Captain Rawlings, "I have decided that I'm coming with you."

"Good show, man!" Rawlings commended, patting him on the back.

"I'll meet you at the head of the road. I must go and collect my horse and weapons and leave word with Colonel Varick. I'll be there as quickly as possible."

The pair clasped hands warmly, and Rawlings climbed back into the saddle as Shelby took off through the buzz of what was left of the encampment. He found the soldier left safeguarding he and Mr. Fox's property and collected his sword and dragoon pistols. He pulled the baldrick over his shoulder and dug into his saddlebag to produce a candle and a dispatch envelope. He ran over to a nearby campfire and lit the candle. Shelby withdrew his notebook and allowed the melted wax to run onto the outer edge of the pages until a thick crust formed. Within a minute, the little notebook was sealed closed and it could not be opened without betraying the invasion. He dropped the journal into the envelope and hurriedly back to the private, asking if he knew the whereabouts of Colonel Varick.

101

"I just saw him, sir. He's right over that-a-way, talking to the staffs of the general officers about the order of march for the withdrawal."

"Excellent. I am going to go speak with him. While I do, go and fetch my horse."

"Yes, sir," the boy soldier saluted and disappeared into the turmoil of the dispersing encampment.

He hated to interrupt the colonel, who was busy giving directions to representatives of generals Poor and Learned. "One moment gentlemen," he said to the officers once he spied Captain Shelby standing respectfully, if impatiently, nearby.

"Hello, Captain." He returned Shelby's salute. "Are your interviews complete?"

"Yes. Thank you for the use of the tent. Colonel, I have decided to help with the relief of Fort Stanwix. I met a friend headed that way and wanted to inform you of my intentions so that you knew where I was, and so that you could report my whereabouts to Mr. Fox should he return before me."

Colonel Varick's eyebrows lifted at the news then his jaw set firmly. "Captain, all of the generals under General Schuyler disagreed with his decision to send the expedition to aid Fort Stanwix; save one. The opposition thinks it foolish to weaken our strength here with Burgoyne only twenty-five miles to our north. But I personally believe that General Schuyler is right; if Stanwix falls, we will face assault here from two sides," he said, again demonstrating his fierce loyalty to his commander. "So I want you to know that I personally appreciate anything you can do to help with the expedition."

"I will do my best, sir. There is one thing you might do for me, though." Shelby hesitated for a moment unsure if he should entrust the journal to Varick. "Look after this for me," he finally said, handing the envelope to the colonel. "If Mr. Fox returns before I do; or if I should fall in this operation, be sure that he gets it."

"You can count on it," Varick said resolutely. He continued, "Captain, the single general who agreed with the General Schuyler has bravely volunteered to lead the force. He just rode out ahead of you to take command. Report directly to him and tell him that I personally sent you."

"Thank you, Colonel. I appreciate your confidence."

"Well, Captain," he smiled. "Your actions fighting under General Alexander are no secret to this command. Your courage and leadership can only be an asset to the mission."

Shelby saluted and turned to leave, but hesitated. "Colonel, who is the general assuming command of the relief force?"

"Benedict Arnold."

Chapter 10

"So, Arnold is in command, eh?" Rawlings commented as he and Shelby rode along.

"Yes. Do you know him?"

"Only by reputation. From what I understand, he is a fierce fighter and brave to the point of recklessness."

Shelby had never met the man personally either, but he was well aware of his exploits. Although from Connecticut, Arnold had distinguished himself in this very region early in the war by capturing Fort Ticonderoga with the help of Ethan Allen and his private army from the Green Mountains. The cannon taken from that fort had then been heroically transported overland by Henry Knox to Boston where their surprise appearance was largely responsible for the British vacating that city. Arnold then commanded the ill-fated invasion of Canada where by sheer force of will he led his men through presumably impassible wilderness. While laying siege to the fortress city of Quebec he sustained a serious leg wound and when the Americans were forced to retreat south, Arnold added naval commander to his list of accomplishments by having a fleet constructed at Lake Champlain to confront the British as they pursued him from Canada. Although the flotilla was defeated in the engagement, Arnold's bold maneuver had delayed the British significantly. Had he not done so, Burgoyne's elaborate plan might not have been necessary as the now contested ground of New York would likely already be in the enemy's hands.

"Hmm," Shelby mused. "Even though Quebec may have ended badly, I suspect we are in good hands if we are to save

Theodore and his companions.   At least we can be confident that Arnold will not err on the side of caution."

"We think alike, William.   From what I hear, St. Leger has a force of 850 Redcoats, Hessians, and Tories plus another 800 Iroquois.   They already defeated a relief force of 800 militia at a place called Oriskany about two weeks ago."

"Yes, General Schuyler told me.   Have you any idea of the disposition of our forces?"

"I hear that Colonel Gansevoort has somewhere around 750 inside the besieged fort.   An equal number of militia, mostly those beaten back at Oriskany, are at Fort Dayton between here and Stanwix, where they are to be met by the 900 from Stillwater."

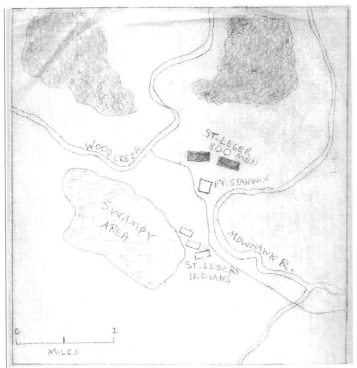

SIEGE OF FORT STANWIX

105

The pair rode through the afternoon and into the evening. A man from Rawlings' unit had kin who lived in the valley of the Mohawk and had given him directions to their farm where they might find lodging for the night.

"Is this it?" Shelby asked, peering through the thickening twilight toward a handsome, if modest house that lay beyond a field of barley which pulsed gently in the evening breeze.

"I suppose it is," Captain Rawlings returned, spurring his horse up the dirt lane.

Light appeared through the windows of the stone hewn house and a wisp of smoke curled from the chimney above the cedar-shingled roof. As they got nearer, Shelby's horse brayed when a half-dozen guinea hen scurried across their path headed toward the nearby vegetable garden to begin their nightly task of picking the leaves clean of insects. Off to their right they could see the outline of a pen and heard the unmistakable snorting of hogs. As if in competition with the pigs, a rambunctious whippoorwill suddenly added his redundant song to the cacophony.

The men rode up close to the house and dismounted. Shelby took hold of his friend's horse and by design positioned himself behind the steeds, his hands on his pistols, should they have been mistaken and this turn out to be an unfriendly household. Rawlings walked up to the door and rapped.

Shelby saw curtains flutter in a downstairs window as a head stealthily spied toward the small landing at the front of the house. A full half minute passed before the portal slowly opened. A small, wizened old man appeared in the crack holding a shotgun.

"What's your business?" he croaked in a gravelly voice.

"Sir, I am sorry to intrude. My name is Captain John Rawlings. I am looking for the home of Ezekiel Hornbeck."

"You've found it," the old man growled back. "But you still ain't answered the question. What's your business?"

Shelby tightened his grip on his pistols.

"My companion and I are riding out to Fort Dayton to help those trapped at Fort Stanwix. A comrade, George Wilks, said that you might afford us a place to stay for the night."

The scowl on the old man's face melted into a broad smile. Shelby thought the transformation magical as the troll-like figure morphed into a cherubic form. He planted the butt of the gun upon the floor. "Goin' out to help at Fort Dayton, are ye? Well, come in. Frank!" he yelled over his shoulder. "Take care of these fellers' horses." A lad of perhaps ten burst through the doorway and snatched the reins from Shelby.

As the soldiers entered the home the family began to materialize from a variety of hiding places. An elderly woman and two small girls came up from the cellar, a young boy inched out from under a table and a middle-aged lady popped from a closet.

"I'm sorry I was rough with ye. My eyesight ain't so sharp anymore and we got to be careful. There's been a fair bit of mischief in these parts of late. So ye know Georgie, huh? Martha," he said to the old woman, "These boys know Georgie." He turned back to Rawlings "Georgie is Martha's sister's, boy. I'm Zeke Hornbeck," the old man exchanged handshakes with the two soldiers.

"We already et, but I can get you a bite if you're hungry," the matron said, coming forward.

Rawlings replied, "That would be very gracious of you, if it's not too much trouble."

"Come on Elizabeth," she said to the mother of the youngsters. "Let's see what we can dig up for these fellers."

Before long the ladies had produced plates piled with cold smoked pork, roasted apples, and the remnants of a delicious pie made with some variety of local berries. Shelby and Rawlings were joined at the kitchen table by the adult members of the household whose stomachs were still full from their dinner, but they were hungry for news of the war.

"This cider is excellent," Shelby commented, seating the mug back on the table before shoveling another piece of meat into his mouth

The patriarch ignored the compliment as he stuffed tobacco into his pipe. "Elizabeth's my daughter," he nodded toward the worried looking woman sitting quietly across the table. "Her husband left with the militia to help them boys at Stanwix but they got ambushed. Luckily he made out alright. He's with them at Fort Dayton. What goes on at Stillwater? Has that rascal Burgoyne made his move yet?"

"No. He's still at Fort Edward," Rawlings replied through forkfuls of pork. "I suspect he's waiting for St. Leger to provide flanking support."

"Over at Fort Dayton, if you run into David Griffin, that's Elizabeth's husband, you tell him that everything's alright here, will ye?" Martha interjected.

"We'll be glad to convey that message if we come upon him," Shelby smiled at Elizabeth.

Ezekiel puffed pensively on his pipe. "If the lobsterbacks take Stanwix, we'll have to skedaddle. It won't be safe here with their Indians running about. The Redcoats ain't much better, though. They won't murder like the savages, but they'll take all of our crops and livestock." His teeth clenched on the stem of his pipe. "We worked too hard this season to let that happen. You boys do your best to stop them, eh?"

"You can count on that, sir." Shelby returned.

It was the following afternoon by the time the pair rode into Fort Dayton. There they found that Captain Rawlings' intelligence on the number of their forces had been fairly accurate. The Continentals from Schuyler's command had been added to the Tryon County militia under General Herkimer. Herkimer had been wounded at the Oriskany ambush, and although he continued to lead his men after the injury, it ultimately resulted in his death eleven days after the engagement.

Shelby and Rawlings dismounted and led their horses along until they found an officer. Both men saluted a major whom Shelby remembered seeing at Stillwater.

"Excuse me, sir," Shelby said. "Can you direct me to General Arnold?"

"He's over yonder, talking with Colonel Willett," he returned, pointing toward a small group of men standing in front of one of the rustic log buildings that populated the inside of the fort.

Shelby thanked the officer and handed the reins of his horse to Captain Rawlings. "Here, I'll be right back. Colonel Varick told me to personally inform the general of our arrival."

As he got closer he had no trouble determining which man was the formidable general. It was neither his uniform nor his insignia that betrayed his rank, but the authoritative bearing and hard penetrating eyes of a commander whose men had no choice but to follow him in combat as he would always be the first into the fray.

The captain advanced and saluted General Arnold directly, ignoring all other officers in the group. Arnold seemed to respect Shelby's directness and turned his cool, pale, gray eyes upon the newcomer as he returned his salute.

"General Arnold, sir. I am Captain Shelby. I and my companion, Captain Rawlings, are here without a unit. We have just ridden in from Stillwater and are anxious to be of any assistance possible. Colonel Varick advised that I report to you directly."

Arnold's high brow creased in apparent admiration of the voluntary efforts of the two captains. "Do you have combat experience?" he asked, clasping his hands behind his back.

"Yes, we both fought in the efforts in Long Island, Brooklyn, and White Plains and I have been with the army in the New Jersey and Pennsylvania since then."

Arnold nodded. "Very well, Captain. We'll find a place for you and your friend. We were just about to hear from Lieutenant Colonel Willett, here. He is second in command at Fort Stanwix and Colonel Gansevoort sent him here to apprise us of the situation. Go on, Colonel," Arnold said, turning to Willett.

"Well, sir, you have the numbers about right. The British have near 900 regulars, including Loyalist militia and the Hessians, and I would say about 800 Iroquois. But it looks like the Indians might abandon the effort, sir." He smiled.

"Is that so?" the general returned, his voice showed interest although his expression remained unchanged.

"Yes, sir. Well you see, when St. Leger sent his Indians and Tories out on that waylay at Oriskany, Colonel Gansevoort had me lead a raid on their empty encampment. We captured or destroyed nearly all of their supplies and equipment. We took twenty-one wagon loads back into the fort with us," he beamed. "The Indians joined up because they were promised that they wouldn't have to do much fighting, but that they'd be able to loot the countryside. They've found things quite different. The Tryon County boys may have had to turn back after Oriskany, but they inflicted pretty heavy casualties on the Indians. When they got back and found that we had stolen back what little booty they had taken on this enterprise, plus all of their own personal property..." he could not help but grin. "Well, word is that they're about ready to abandon the fight and turn tail for home. St. Leger is trying to convince them otherwise, but they're disconcerted, and in no mood for another fight."

The corner of the dark-haired general's mouth flitted momentarily and a gleam seemed to flash in those gray eyes but Shelby could not tell if this was the result of the strategic advantage that might result from an Indian withdrawal or if the

110

pugnacious man had had a mere visceral response to the word "fight."

An officer interjected, "Is it true that St. Leger warned that he would unleash his Indians to kill women and children if Gansevoort did not surrender the fort?"

Apparently Arnold took no offense at the outburst as he stared at Willett, waiting for the man's reply.

"To be sure. After the column was turned back at Oriskany, St. Leger thought that we would give up. He sent a major in under a white flag with a message. It said that if we did not capitulate he would not be able to control his Indians and they would massacre all in the fort and then head into the valley murdering all they encountered, including women and children. Under Colonel Gansevoort's orders I composed the reply myself; informing Mr. St. Leger that no officer with any sense of honor would convey such a degrading message and that he may do his best to take the fort as he would not have it handed to him."

"It seems St. Leger accepted the challenge," Willett continued, "as he began building redoubts and digging trenches closer to the fort. Colonel Gansevoort dispatched myself and Lieutenant Stockwell," he nodded to the man next to him, "to make our way here for help. It was two nights of hard travel through the swamps, for we dared not take to the roads nor travel by daylight, but here we are-- and thankfully here you are. God bless General Schuyler for sending you."

"And soon St. Leger will rue his folly," Arnold remarked. "Let's go inside and have a look at that map," he said to Willett and Stockwell as he stepped toward the little log building.

"Have you eaten today, Captain?" an officer in the small group asked Shelby.

"I suppose you heard my stomach growling," Shelby joked back. "No sir, neither I nor my companion have had anything today. A hospitable farmer provided us with dinner last night but we left before breakfast."

111

"The commissary is over there," he pointed. "Why don't you gentlemen replenish your strength. I'm Colonel Miller. I'm acting as aide to General Arnold here at Fort Dayton. We lost two captains at Oriskany. Would you and Captain Rawlings be opposed to leading militia companies in the assault?"

"Not at all. We will serve in whatever capacity we are needed."

"Excellent. I will be sure to find you in ample time before our departure to show you to your men. Now go and get something to eat," he smiled, "that time I *did* hear your stomach growl."

The next morning dawned without any respite from the unpleasant humidity that hung over the wilds of New York that August. Shelby and Rawlings broke their nightly fast with some biscuits and coffee. As they ate, amiably chatting with some new acquaintances the bustle about the camp indicated that the operation was in preparation. Following their short meal the pair borrowed a razor, enabling them to wash and shave.

"Captains," Colonel Miller announced his presence as Rawlings hurriedly toweled the soapy water from his face.

"Sir," they replied, jumping to attention and saluting.

Returning their salute Colonel Miller continued. "I have your men assembled. If you will follow me, I will make the introductions."

They trailed the officer to an area where two companies stood next to one another. They were both in formation, although informally chatting with one another. The men all wore civilian clothes and were outfitted with a variety of weaponry. Most carried hunting rifles typical of the non-professional soldier, but many held muskets captured in some skirmish or bought by wealthier towns when their own militia units were formed. Some of the men carrying the muskets also owned the accompanying bayonet, while others merely

112

possessed the gun itself. As the officers arrived someone called out "Attention!" and the citizen-soldiers did their best to assume the more formal military posture.

A man came forward from each of the ranks and approached the trio, exchanging salutes. Colonel Miller stated, "Captain Rawlings, you'll be leading Company C in the assault. "This is Sergeant Schaffer," he said of the short, stocky, bushy eye-browed soldier. Rawlings and his new second-in-command exchanged greetings, and the militiaman was introduced to Shelby as well.

The other man was of average height and build, but was distinctive due to his bright orange hair and freckled face. "Captain Shelby, this is Sergeant McGillis of Company D." The same procedure was followed and both captains traded salutations with the part-time soldier.

Colonel Miller went on to discuss the disposition of each company and queried both sergeants as to the background and experience of the men for the benefit of their new commanders. As this conversation progressed, the figure of General Arnold appeared. He was about forty yards away conversing with a militiaman. Shelby tried to focus on the discourse at hand, but impulsively peaked over toward the general, noticing that he and the other man had been joined by a scout. The newest man's back was to the captain, but the gesticulations of his hands and movements of his body indicated that he was trying to persuade Arnold on some point. Again Shelby's eyes returned to the colonel and sergeants but after a minute's time a compulsion forced him to steal another look past them back toward Arnold. He saw the general nodding and then the buckskin clad scout waved his arm in a come-hither motion. Two soldiers advanced, escorting a third man. They passed rather close to Shelby and he was afforded a good look at the prisoner's face. He was unsure if the man was a simpleton or deranged, but it was clear from his facial features that he was not in full possession of his faculties.

113

When the guards delivered their charge, the conversation between the general and the woodsman continued. Several Onieda Indians allied with the Patriots were brought into the discussion and it was only then that the scout turned enough for Shelby to view his face. He let out an audible gasp as he recognized his partner, Mr. Fox.

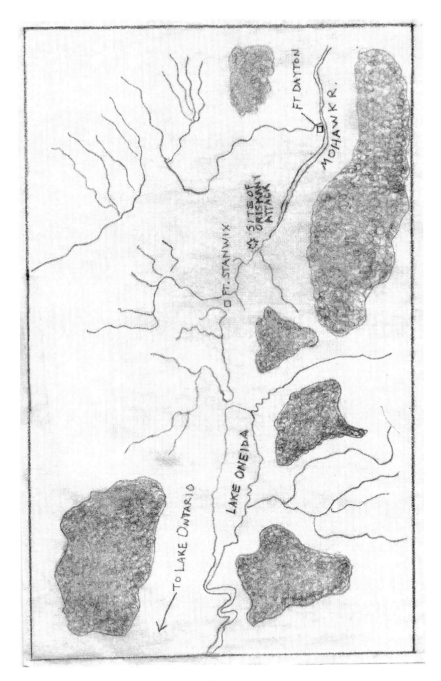

FT. DAYTON

MOHAWK R.

SITE OF
ORISKANY
ATTACK

FT. STANWIX

LAKE ONEIDA

TO LAKE ONTARIO

115

Chapter 11

Shelby was as polite and centered as he could manage during the remainder of the discussion with the non-commissioned officers of the militia companies but inwardly he bristled with impatience. His eyes kept darting past Colonel Miller and the militiamen, determined to keep his investigative partner in sight. Luckily Fox's meeting with Arnold continued as his own confab ended. "So, when marching orders are given, I will convey them to you gentlemen," Colonel Miller said to Shelby and Rawlings. "And you can form up your men again at that time."

"It was good to meet you sergeant. And you sergeant," Shelby hastily returned the salutes of the two men. "Um Colonel," he stepped after Miller as the man began walking toward General Arnold. As Colonel Miller paused, Shelby turned to Rawlings, "I'll meet up with you shortly, John," and left his confused friend to walk alongside the colonel.

"Something I can help you with, Captain?" he asked as they went.

Shelby considered whether he should open up to the man, and if so, how much he should say. He began, "Well Colonel, I..." but was cut off as General Arnold's meeting dispersed and Mr. Fox and Arnold headed off in opposite directions. "That man is a colleague of mine," Shelby pointed toward the figure of the retreating woodsman. "I need to speak with him."

"Oh. He just came in this morning and wanted desperately to meet with the general. He said that he had some information that might be of great importance regarding the attack on St. Leger's forces and insisted on speaking to the general directly.

116

Apparently they know one another." Colonel Miller stopped. "I need to report to the general, so I will be in touch when I have the marching orders," he said before splitting off to follow Arnold's path.

Shelby hurried after his partner, trying to keep his eye on the buckskin clad figure through the commotion inside the fort. Men, wagons, horses, alternately obscured his view. He scurried ahead, banging forcefully into two Indians. Some of their grotesque war-paint had come off on his sleeve and he tried to rub it away while continuing on the trail of the imposter trapper. Fortunately he caught sight of Mr. Fox as he turned the corner of one of the log buildings. As the pursuing captain rounded the cabin, he gasped suddenly as he was grabbed by the shoulders and thrown against the side of the building.

"Captain, Shelby? What in heaven's name are you doing here?" his attacker asked, the familiar half-smile curling his lips.

"Mr. Fox!" he exhaled in relief. "I was hoping to catch up with you to pose the very same question!"

Fox released hold of his partner and laughed in that silent manner of his. He patted at the rumpled shoulders of Shelby's uniform. "I'm sorry, Captain. My intuition has become attuned to suspicion and I sensed that someone was following me. Had I known it was you, I would not have treated you so roughly."

"Oh, that's quite alright," Shelby smiled back. "But what are you doing here? And are you alright?" he winced at the bruising on his partner's face.

"Perhaps we can find a quiet corner and exchange stories over a cup of coffee," the investigator suggested.

The duo visited the commissary and settled in an unpopulated area to catch each other up on events. Captain Shelby went first, describing how he came to be at Fort Dayton.

Fox took a sip of coffee and when the clay cup descended from his mouth it revealed that characteristic crooked smirk.

"So, you disobeyed my orders to stay in the encampment at Stillwater. Ah, don't waste your time with justifications," he held up a hand to cut off the captain as Shelby's mouth opened sheepishly. "I approve whole heartedly," he remarked as a confused expression spread across Shelby's face. "You're learning, Captain. You're learning!" he laughed. "How could I be cross with you? You disregarded my orders because they conflicted with your conscience. Your morality would not allow you to sit idly by while a friend's life was in jeopardy."

Shelby's brow knitted. He welcomed the fact that Mr. Fox accepted his actions but was also fully aware that as a soldier he had acted inappropriately.

Mr. Fox tapped into his unique powers as he appeared to read his companion's thoughts. "Don't let it trouble you, lad," he said affectionately. "You prudently left your journal for me back with Colonel Varick, so you did not neglect our mission. And although I am in charge of our investigation, I am not your superior officer. You did not really breach your military oath. And I know you well enough to say with certainty that should you decide not to follow an order it would only be in extreme circumstances, and when you were positive it was in the best interest of your men and our war effort."

"So," Fox diverted the subject back to their assignment, "what did you find out in your interviews?"

Shelby instantly shifted away from his internal conflict and recited all he could about his interrogations, excusing himself if he did not remember all of the specifics from memory. He assured Mr. Fox that he would consult his notebook upon their return to the Hudson encampment to be sure he had not left out any important facets.

"You did well, Captain," the investigator complimented. Fox pushed up the leather hunting cap and scratched his head pensively. "So, the boy said that the women left of their own accord… That is interesting," he mused. "And the leader of the Indians was called *Le Loup?*"

"Yes. And he wore black paint over his torso and head with a white lightning bolt diagonally traversing his face," Shelby stated in an attempt to impress his partner with the details and reassure that his recollection of the interrogations was sound.

"Hmm," Fox pondered for a moment. "And we have conflicting opinions on the romance between Miss McCrea and Lieutenant Jones. The married couple believes that they were truly in love, but the washerwoman thinks otherwise, citing some mysterious meetings with an older fellow." Fox looked up at Shelby. "Did any man fitting the description live in the vicinity?"

"I believe that if one did, she would have named him as the guilty party. The woman seemed to enjoy gossip and I have no doubt that she would have made the leap to implicate if a neighbor bore resemblance; despite not clearly seeing the man."

"Did you ask the others if they knew anyone fitting the description?" Fox pressed.

"No," Shelby shook his head regretfully. "I had already dismissed them. Mrs. Braithwaite was the last person I interviewed."

"Hmm," Fox mused. "We shall have to follow up on that when we get back. Fort Edward is hardly a teeming metropolis but it is possible that such a person lived in the area unknown to this washerwoman.

Mr. Fox quickly shifted his tact. "And you say the married couple feels as if Miss McCrea's brother, Colonel McCrea disliked Lieutenant Jones?"

Shelby pondered the question. "I don't think *dislike* accurately describes their opinion. I believe they said that that the engagement made Colonel McCrea *uneasy* and that he did not approve of the match."

119

"That could be no more than the concern of an over-protective brother *or* the animus a Patriot would feel toward a Tory." He scratched his chin. "It is really unfortunate that we did not get to speak with Colonel McCrea," he said to himself.

"Does any of this information help? It seems to only further muddy the water," Shelby commented, taking another swig of his coffee.

"You have added more pieces to the puzzle. But we still must figure how they fit together."

"Did you find anything of interest at Fort Edward?" Shelby asked, "And what are you doing *here*?" he queried, having become so engrossed in the McCrea mystery he had nearly forgotten his partner's inexplicable appearance.

Mr. Fox chuckled silently. "Both are fair questions. Let me tell you of Fort Edward first. He began by describing his exhumation of the girl's corpse but his partner interrupted his account.

"So you examined the body?" a surprised Shelby asked.

"Yes. I felt it necessary." Fox continued unfazed, "Her head was cleaved with a tomahawk and she was scalped, but she was also shot through the head. I had hoped to determine her cause of death beyond question but I could not do so," he shook his head in mild consternation. "It seems likely that the tomahawk wound was the death blow and that the bullet was a postmortem wound meant to cover the murder by portraying the killing as the inadvertent act of the militia. I thought that if this were the case, that the shot would have been taken up close and that I would find powder residue upon her hair. But I found none."

"So you believe that the militia did in fact kill her? If so, why the tomahawk wound?"

"It is still a possibility that the militia shot her, and she was still alive though mortally wounded and then one of the savages ended her life with his tomahawk and took the scalp."

"However," Fox continued, "It is also still possible that she was murdered by the Indians and the bullet wound is a deception to implicate the militia. Indians are a scheming lot and I would not put it past them to deviously fire that shot into the corpse from a few meters away in order to prevent powder-scarring on the skull."

Shelby took another sip of coffee. "So we're no closer to knowing the truth," he frustratingly commented.

"I would not say that."

The captain looked up, surprised.

Fox's shoulders shook as he quietly chortled at his companion's reaction. "Although I am not sure if she was killed by the Indians or the militia, or even another party entirely, I believe that it was most definitely an act of calculated murder."

"Why? What leads you to believe so?" Shelby sputtered.

Mr. Fox smirked as he removed the vials from his bag and handed them to his partner. "I found these hidden in the McCrea cabin. I had to tussle with a Hessian fellow to get them," he gingerly touched his bruised face. "The one bottle contains cobalt chloride; the other glycerine. When mixed with water they produce an invisible ink."

Shelby looked up from the vials, a shocked expression on his face.

Fox continued, "One usually writes a normal looking letter and then applies the hidden message between the visible lines, or around the margin. If heat is then applied to the paper, the secret writing will materialize in blue but vanish again when the warmth is removed."

"Do you mean to suggest that Miss McCrea was a spy?" the captain asked in an astonished tone.

"That might explain the clandestine assignations with the stooped man."

Shelby was still dumbfounded at the possibility. "Who was she spying *for*?"

121

The half-grin returned to Fox's lips. "I have no idea. But I intend to pursue it," he stated deliberately. "Oh, and as to your second question. How I came to be here at Fort Dayton is another matter entirely."

It took a moment for Shelby to shake off his amazement over the apparent occupation of the murdered woman. Finally Mr. Fox's words registered with him. "Oh yes. If it is half as interesting as your last tale I suspect you shall overwhelm me once again," he smiled.

Mr. Fox smirked back. "After I left Fort Edward, I recrossed the Hudson and swung out wide of Saratoga. As I began south again I ran into a group of men heading here."

"More militia?" Shelby asked.

"Not exactly," Mr. Fox drained the last bit of coffee from his cup and then continued. "They were kin to a captured Tory named Hon Yost Schuyler."

"Schuyler?"

Fox nodded. "Yes, he is a distant relation to the general and a nephew of General Herkimer."

"The commander of the Tryon County militia force attacked at Oriskany," Shelby confirmed.

"The same. He has just died from the wounds received in that ambush."

"Yes, I heard. So go on, what of these men you came across near Saratoga."

"They were on their way here to bargain for Hon Yost's release. He is mentally defective and they were hoping General Arnold might show some pity and pardon their kinsman."

A shadow crossed Shelby's face. "I'm sorry. I must be missing something. How do these events bring *you* to Fort Dayton?"

Mr. Fox laughed quietly. "Where you and I recognize lunacy as a defect, the Indians usually see it as some communication with the Great Spirit. You see, in the last war I

122

was once party to a ploy using an insane chap to convince a band of Huron to abandon the field. When I heard of this Hon Yost fellow, I thought I might suggest a similar ruse and see if we could not get St. Leger's savages to give up the siege and head back to Canada. I proposed that we allow the man his freedom if he were to help us. He could be allowed to 'escape' to St. Leger's lines and tell our enemies that Arnold is on the way with an *overwhelming* force. A few of the Oneidas allied with us could go along to corroborate the tale. This Hon Yost could also tell the Indians that the Great Spirit foresees their doom should they stay and fight."

"From what I understand they are fairly dispirited already," Shelby smiled. "While they were off attacking Hermiker's force at Oriskany, men from Fort Stanwix stole all of their goods."

"Yes, I have heard that too. I was hoping that one final push on their confidence might be enough to get them to leave the siege."

"So I take it that General Arnold agreed to the plan?" asked the captain.

"He did, but it was a delicate matter to convince him."

"How do you mean?"

"He is not an easy man to deal with."

"Some have said the same of you," Shelby needled.

Fox smirked guiltily. "Yes, and they are right. I am hardheaded and I insist upon doing things my own way. However, General Arnold is different."

"How so?"

Mr. Fox exhaled, as if he were considering how best to explain. "He is brave and he is cunning, but his ego is easily bruised. *How* things are presented to Arnold are as important as *what* is presented. For someone like me, this creates a problem. I make no pretense to possessing a cajoling nature and he and I have had our differences before."

123

"Oh, so you know him personally?" Shelby commented, surprised at the ever growing number of luminaries with whom the plain Quaker gentleman had ties.

"Yes," he returned curtly and without further comment.

Fox had disappeared for the rest of the night and as the column headed out of the Fort Dayton toward Stanwix the next morning, Shelby wondered what had become of his partner. He rode alongside of the marching militia company he commanded, Rawlings in a similar position some thirty yards behind him. The expedition was nearing its destination when the call to halt echoed back down the column. Shelby looked around curiously and then stood up in his stirrups. Up ahead he could make out the mounted figures of General Arnold and Lieutenant Colonel Willett who were suddenly joined by the half-witted Hon Yost and from another quarter appeared the mounted figure of Mr. Fox. The discussion lasted for five minutes, after which time the advance resumed.

Shelby had made no mention of the proposed ruse to his friend Rawlings, or anyone else, knowing the necessity of secrecy for such an operation. As he trotted along his mind swam, wondering if the renewal of the march meant that the trick had failed. Much to his relief, he spied his investigative partner riding back down the column in his direction.

"Mr. Fox!" he called out, raising his hand. The man smiled in recognition and reigned up alongside the captain.

"Is there news? Did the subterfuge work?" he asked anxiously.

The Mona Lisa smile flitted across Fox's mouth. "Better than expected. That half-wit sold it completely. They believe that our numbers are more than three thousand; nearly triple what we truly have. The Indians abandoned St. Leger, but not before turning on the British and raiding their supplies. The

124

Redcoats are equally unnerved. General St. Leger has abandoned the siege. He is retreating toward Canada."

"That is fantastic!" Captain Shelby beamed.

"We are moving on to the fort where Arnold plans on releasing a detachment to pursue St. Leger's forces, thinking he might carve them up on the run."

"Your friend, Lieutenant Vanderslyke-- Was that his name? He appears to be out of harm's way."

"Indeed. I am of course grateful of that, but more importantly, the second arm of Burgoyne's three pronged attack has just been eliminated!" Shelby nearly exclaimed. "First Howe abandoned him and now St. Leger." The realization dawned on the young officer like a ray of sunshine bursting through the clouds. For the first time, it appeared that the Americans had a real chance at defeating General Burgoyne.

Chapter 12

"William? John?" Theodore Vanderslyke's mouth was agape at the sight of his friends. "By God, it's good to see you! What are you doing here?" he asked, warmly embracing the pair. With a broad smile Rawlings replied, "We heard that you had your backside in the ringer once more. William said that we should let you suffer the fate of one with such poor judgment, but I said, 'He's not a bad chap, I think we should go and save him.'"

Shelby sprang to his defense, "I said no such thing! If I recall properly, John stated that you still owed him a few shillings from a game of dice back on Long Island and the skinflint insisted that we relieve the fort so that he could collect," he fended off his friend's jest with his own.

"Well, fortunately you did not have to risk your life to collect," Vanderslyke returned to Rawlings. "St. Leger has run away!"

"Of course he did," Rawlings replied. "He heard that William and I were on the way," he winked.

"It's inexplicable really. Just a few days ago he sent a messenger into the fort warning that if we didn't surrender, we would all be slaughtered by his Indians. Now, his whole force is in retreat!" The lieutenant shook his head in disbelief.

"We can explain that," Shelby stated. He went on to describe the ruse. Remembering Mr. Fox's description of Arnold's fragile ego, he was careful to credit the scheme to the general. He then explained the true story as to how he and Rawlings met up at Stillwater and how they hurried out to join the expedition to relieve Fort Stanwix.

126

Lieutenant Vanderslyke was visibly warmed by the actions of his friends. He patted each on the back and shook their hands once more, openly expressing his gratitude.

"So you've been sent to report on the McCrea murder," Vanderslyke said to Shelby in a more somber tone. "Bad business, that." He shook his head. "Where is this Mr. Fox? You said that he accompanied you here, correct?"

"General Arnold is collecting a force to pursue St. Leger and Mr. Fox is finding a scout for the general."

The three friends spent the afternoon within the confines of Fort Stanwix. Into the evening the trio sat around a small fire, laughing and reminiscing. The time was a pleasant distraction from the hardships and horrors that make war such a hideous endeavor. Although unsaid, the comrades were well aware that given the violent times, they might never have this opportunity again.

The following morning Arnold was busy giving orders to the detachment that was to chase down St. Leger. He had decided to leave two companies of militia at the fort to reinforce the garrison before marching the rest of the men back to the base on the Hudson. The militia companies to remain at Stanwix were those that had been put under Shelby and Rawlings, but of course those two men could not stay. Rawlings was due back with his own unit and Shelby had to continue with the investigation. Mr. Fox had decided that they should head out ahead of Arnold's force. He was eager to get back to the Hudson encampment and follow up on the clue of Jane McCrea's secretive meetings with her elderly associate. Captain Rawlings chose to travel back with Shelby and Fox rather than endure the slow pace of the marching column.

The three men followed the Mohawk eastward, toward the main American base along the Hudson. The weather was warm but the close proximity of the river allowed them to water their horses and fill their canteens at regular intervals.

"Mr. Fox, didn't you also have a mule when you left Stillwater?" Shelby asked, sure not to mention his partner's destination or objective in the query. Although he trusted Rawlings implicitly, he had no right to divulge any more of their mission than the simple fact that they were compiling a report on the girl's death.

"Right you are, Captain. I handed it over to General Arnold at Fort Dayton. He had a small artillery piece that was in want of a beast to pull it. His column will bring it back to Stillwater upon their return."

"It won't do any good at Stillwater," Shelby slyly commented.

"Oh? Why not?" Fox asked flatly.

"Because General Schuyler has pulled back to the islands where the Mohawk and Hudson converge," Shelby said, quietly savoring possessing some information unknown to the clever investigator.

"The Sprouts?" Fox returned.

"That's right," Shelby reminded himself aloud, "you are familiar with the area."

"I suppose it is a good defensive maneuver given that he sent nine hundred of his men on the mission to relieve Stanwix." Fox judged, ignoring Shelby's comment.

"Captain Rawlings," Fox turned to Shelby's friend.

"Yes?"

"I find it interesting that you did not join up as a privateer. How is it you came to be in the army rather than the navy?"

A look of puzzlement clouded the face of Captain Rawlings but it quickly faded as if a revelation had reached his mind. "I suppose that William here has told of my background."

Shelby laughed. "No, I mentioned our times on Long Island and White Plains, but nothing of your personal history."

"Then how is it you suspect that it more likely that I am apt to be a seaman than a soldier?" he asked, the quizzical expression returning.

Fox's half-grin danced across his lips. "You are a young man, but you have considerable wrinkles around your eyes. This is a characteristic of one who is habitually forced to squint due to the sun's glint off of a body of water. Also, the leather of your boots is bleached where it meets the soles. That is the result of long exposure to saltwater. However, most telling are the knots that you have used on the straps of your cartridge box and rifle. Those are knots used by sailors."

"Well Mr. Fox, You are quite observant," Rawlings laughed. "I think it only fair to assuage your curiosity about my choice of martial career. You are correct that my pre-war days were spent amidst saltwater, but I am not a sailor in the sense you might imagine. I grew up in the southern part of New Jersey along the Delaware Bay. My family tended the oyster beds. I was on the bay most of my life, but usually no more than a few hundred yards from shore. We use the knots of sailors in our trade but I have never been to sea."

"Ah, that explains it." Fox laughed noiselessly. "Thank you for satisfying my curiosity. I have been plagued by an inquisitive nature that simply demands explanation," he joked.

That night the trio found themselves upon the doorstep of the Hornbeck farm. The lethargic pooch reclined in the same spot as the soldiers' earlier visit, unwilling to even raise its head enough to meet Rawlings' attempt to give him a scratch. Like their first stop at the homestead, Ezekiel Hornbeck's shotgun peeked through the door to greet them, but when the codger recognized his visitors, his cautious demeanor melted into genuine congeniality and he welcomed the men inside.

The family was eager for news of the relief effort. They were thrilled to hear of the mission's success and although disappointed that Shelby and Rawlings had not come across

129

Elizabeth's husband at the fort, they were assured that he was probably fine as the coup that had liberated Fort Stanwix had been a bloodless one.

The farmer's hospitality did not disappoint as he was happy to put up the men on their return trip. Luckily they were in time for dinner so the trio joined the family for a bountiful and delicious meal they knew they were unlikely to see again in the foreseeable future.

The following morning the men were not allowed to depart before Mrs. Hornbeck and her daughter served them a hearty breakfast. The news of the departure of the British, and more importantly to the farmers of the valley, of the Indians, had left the family in a celebratory mood and they insisted on providing the men with a sumptuous feast before they left. The sun had been up for two hours before the grateful, though impatient party was able to ride away from the farmhouse.

The men rode three abreast upon the wide road that ran about a hundred yards inland of the Mohawk River. The interval between the river and the road was a wooded one, but patches of open meadow occupied the other side. Shelby was nearest the river, Rawlings in the center and Mr. Fox flanked the right side.

"I have not eaten that well in a long while," Fox commented, glancing back over his shoulder as if the farm were not miles behind them.

"Indeed," laughed Rawlings. "As you know we dined there on our way out to Dayton, but we had missed dinner. Although those scraps would put any army food to shame, I am glad that we were fortunate enough to sample the cooking at regular meal time."

"The relief they feel regarding the removal of the savages is warranted," Fox said gravely, the animus he held toward the Indians evident in his voice. Just as quickly however, his somber tone faded. "I suspect that Mrs. Hornbeck is of Dutch stock. No woman makes a breakfast like a Dutch woman.

Those crullers!" Mr. Fox licked his lips at the thought of the sweet rolls served up at the farmhouse.

"I believe you to be correct," laughed Rawlings. "When I was at Fort Montgomery, it seemed the whole area was populated by the descendants of the original Dutch settlers. Most of our pay seemed to go to the pastries conjured up by the local girls—or the beer brewed by their husbands," he chuckled.

"Oh Captain," Fox called past Rawlings to Shelby. "It appears that the farm boy did not secure your saddle well enough." He pointed to the buckle on the girth straps where the prong of the buckle was not fully through the hole. If the horse gave one good jolt, the tine would surely slip free causing the saddle and rider to fall from the mount's back.

Shelby bent over to look at the strap and as he did so a booming crack echoed through the air. All three of the Patriots were intimately familiar with the distinctive sound of a rifle shot and the natural maneuver would have been to spur their horses into a gallop. However, the precarious situation of Shelby's saddle prevented such an action so the men tumbled from the right side of their mounts to put their horses between them and the shooter.

"It came from that way; along the river bank," Shelby hissed, peering over his saddle in the direction of the Mohawk.

"Yes," whispered back Fox. "Captain…"

"What is it Mr. Fox?" Shelby asked in a distracted, hushed tone as he sought to spy the shooter.

"Captain, you had better come here."

Shelby scanned the woods once more and then crept around the rear of his friend's horse. He gasped when he saw Rawlings upon the ground, a large red stain growing on his abdomen. Mr. Fox cradled the man's head in the crook of his arm.

"My God! John!" He scurried to the man's side.

"Just a scratch," his friend joked. He coughed, and a trickle of blood ran out of the corner of his mouth.

131

"You take him," Fox ordered. "We're still in danger. Drag him into the tall grass," he said as he jerked his head toward the meadow that bordered the right side of the road. "You'll be hidden from view there. I'll be back." With that Fox disappeared into the woods across the road, rifle in hand.

Shelby grabbed his friend from behind, hooking his forearms under the man's armpits. He dared not stand, but stayed as low as possible, crawling in a backward crouch as he pulled Rawlings into the protective blind of the prairie grass.

Meanwhile Fox skulked silently through the forest. It was obvious that Shelby had been the target and had only avoided death when he had leaned over to examine his saddle strap. Unfortunately, the ball had continued past its intended victim, striking Captain Rawlings. Without thought, his mind calculated the trajectory of the bullet knowing that the shooter must have been stationed in a tree ahead of them and to their left. It was a matter of moments before he found an oak with a broken lower limb and bark scraped from its trunk. The experienced woodsman immediately identified the spot where someone had descended in a hurry.

Caution was essential, as the assassin could still be lurking, waiting to make good on his murderous goal. Fox scanned the woods, focusing not only his uncanny eyesight on the depths of the forest, but his hearing as well. The flutter of every leaf, the chirp of every bird, the drop of each acorn upon the mossy floor, were all sifted through his senses as he searched the surroundings. Satisfied that the assassin was not in the vicinity, he focused his attention on the base of the oak, quickly finding the trail of the sniper. Rapidly, though soundlessly, he followed signs that would have escaped the eyes of most white men. He traced the trail through the woods, emerging at the bank of the Mohawk.

"Do not move!" he called out as he peered down the barrel of his rifle at a man just about to step into a canoe. The felon was about fifty feet away, his back to Fox. The man complied, dropping the gun he held in his left hand. "Raise your hands!" Fox approached slowly. "Turn around!" he ordered. As the sniper obeyed, Fox's lip curled knowingly as he recognized the ambusher who had now three times tried to end their lives.

Fox moved to within ten feet of the villain. "Keep your hands up."

"I'm tryin' but I've a shoulder wound, as I'm sure you're aware," he replied fiercely.

Who are you?" Fox asked through clenched teeth.

He coldly replied, "My name would mean nothin' to you."

"I will then pose a question that means quite a lot to me: Why are you trying to kill us?"

"For the same reason I've done many things. For money."

"You are a hired assassin, eh?" Fox's half-grin was a sardonic one. "An agent of both murder *and* mammon," he scoffed. "Although I am certain that God would not welcome you into his kingdom, I am prepared to give you the opportunity to apply for admission in person. Give me the name of your employer or you will know the answer posthaste."

"Mr. Fox!" Shelby called out, emerging from the fringe of the woods adjacent to the sniper. "John is dead!" he said, as he crunched through the brush, closing on the killer.

Fox glanced over toward his approaching partner who suddenly let loose with one of his dragoon pistols. The blast echoed across the river, bouncing back from the trees that lined the opposite bank. The assassin collapsed, tumbling upon his face. Mr. Fox ran over to the fallen foe, joined immediately by Shelby.

"Captain, that was beyond foolish," he snapped, turning the man over to reveal that he was stone dead. "I can understand your desire for vengeance over the killing of your friend, but now you too are a cold-blooded murderer! And, this man admitted that he was paid to slay us. We needed to find out who hired him. By heavens you have acted imprudently!"

Shelby had waited solemnly during his companion's rant. "Mr. Fox," he said gravely.

"What?" he returned, his voice thick with uncharacteristic exasperation.

Shelby did not reply, rather he knelt by the dead man's hand, unclenching it to reveal the blade of a throwing knife, the handle of which was still hidden up the man's sleeve.

The investigator's eyes widened at the sight, suddenly aware that with the man's hands held aloft, as they had been, a well timed flick of the wrist could have put the weapon squarely into Fox's chest.

"You are right in thinking that I wanted revenge upon the man," Shelby said quietly. "And although I hope that I would not have, I may have killed him in retribution. However, I never got that far. The reason I shot him was so that I would not lose *two* friends today."

Chapter 13

Captain Shelby and Mr. Fox agreed that the meadow was a suitable place to inter their departed colleague. The investigator was still in possession of the entrenching shovel he had taken with him to Fort Edward and for the second time that week it was used not to build a rampart or dig a foxhole but rather to attend to one who had left this world.

As Shelby removed the last bit of earth from the rectangular fissure, Mr. Fox appeared with a cross he had fashioned from two hickory branches. The makeshift marker had been sharpened at its base with precise strokes from the Quaker's tomahawk. He pushed it into the ground at the head of the plot and then used the reverse side of his Indian weapon to bang it firmly into place.

Without comment the pair lowered Captain Rawlings into the aperture. They looked upon him for a long moment before Shelby turned to his partner and said, "Mr. Fox, would you mind saying a few words?"

The devout man would have said his own prayer silently anyway, but he was touched that Shelby held him in high enough regard to make such a request. Long before, he had spent many hours in quiet contemplation laboring to compose a benediction appropriate for fallen comrades. The fruit of those efforts was unfortunately burned in his memory, having recited the short but solemn speech more times than he could count in the course of two wars.

"Lord, we ask that you forgive our friend his transgressions and accept him into your heavenly kingdom. Although you have taught us to show amity to one another, our brother took up arms only to defend the meek and spread your vision of equity and tranquility. His sword is laid down forever and we ask that you now grant him the peace he fought to achieve in this world."

"Amen," Shelby said before making the sign of the cross in the tradition of the Catholic faith.

A cloth was placed over Captain Rawlings' still handsome face before the pair somberly pulled the earth into the grave, lying to rest another child of the American Revolution.

Fox had thoroughly searched the deceased assassin but had found nothing of importance upon the man. He had begun to suggest that they bury him as well, but stopped short when a look of hate materialized in Shelby's eyes. The captain would have preferred to leave the corpse for the wolves, but his heart thawed enough that he acquiesced to a middle ground. He and Mr. Fox stuffed river rocks into the man's clothing and draped him over the remains of a large fallen sycamore limb about six feet long and ten inches in diameter. Mr. Fox then floated the log out into the Mohawk, the slumped form hanging over it at its midsection. The investigator waded out into deeper water, pushing his cargo in front of him. The current tugged at the arms of the corpse, pulling them outward until they were over the villain's head in a cruel pantomime of his actual position the moment he was killed. Fox lifted one end and the murderer slid slowly down the smooth, barkless wood until he tumbled off, disappearing into his watery grave.

*   *   *

"Who goes there?" asked a young, though hard-faced soldier stationed as a picket a mile outside of the encampment.

"I am Captain Shelby and this is Mr. Fox. We were with General Arnold and are returning from Fort Stanwix."

"What's the watchword?" he asked.

136

"As I said, we were off with Arnold, but the one given me before we left was 'Jupiter.'"

The private eyed them suspiciously, but shouldered his firearm. "What's the news from Stanwix?" he asked.

"The news is good. St. Leger has abandoned the fort. He and his Indians are retreating toward Canada. General Arnold has ordered a pursuit and hopes to destroy the British before they escape."

"Alright. It seems as though you're on the level," the inexperienced youth returned. "We had an official messenger come through with the news several hours ago," he stated, inexplicably giving confirmation of the expedition's success more validity than the password.

"Oh, so General Schuyler knows already?" Shelby asked.

"Schuyler?" He shook his head. "General Schuyler's gone. But I'm sure General Gates has been informed." The sentry let them pass and the pair moved on toward the encampment.

"So Gates has arrived," Shelby said almost to himself.

"Do you know him?" Fox asked.

"Barely. He was with us for a few days before Trenton but claimed illness and did not participate in the attack. Instead he went to Baltimore to confer with Congress."

"And you?" Shelby smiled at his partner, "It seems as if you are acquainted with everyone of importance."

"During the last war he was stationed at several of the forts in the Mohawk Valley and I was through most of them, but I don't remember ever meeting him."

"On which of 'the Sprouts' do you suppose we will find General Gates?" Shelby asked.

"None I should suspect." Fox chuckled in that silent manner of his. "The Sprouts are the channels of the Mohawk that cut around the islands forming a type of delta where it empties into the Hudson. I believe that we will find him on Van Schaick's Island. It is the best location for an encampment and I doubt that

137

Gates could pass up using the Van Schaick Mansion as a headquarters."

Shelby nodded, mindless of the jest made at his ignorance of the area. "Will we need a ferry?" he asked, glancing back at Rawlings' recently purchased horse trailing behind his own.

"No. I know the fords. Some are quite shallow. We will have no trouble."

Mr. Fox had proved correct. The new commander had set up shop in the spacious Van Schaick House and the rest of the army was bivouacked in fields not far from the mansion.

As they entered the camp, Shelby stopped a man with a sergeant's insignia. "Can you direct me to Colonel Varick, please?"

"Yes sir," he saluted. "He's over in that tent," he pointed. "He's none too happy, though, so I'd watch myself, sir."

"Thank you," he dismissed the soldier and the pair made a beeline for the large tent, much like the one Shelby had used to conduct his interviews.

"Colonel Varick?" Shelby called inside. "It is I, Captain Shelby."

"Shelby? Come in!"

The men slid through the flap to find the colonel seated at a table, quill in hand, a series of ledgers and books spread out before him. Shelby and the man exchanged salutes.

"I'm glad to see that you have made it back in one piece," he smiled, although somewhat wearily. "And Mr. Fox, you have returned as well," he said, apparently oblivious of the Quaker's bruised face. The colonel stood and walked over to a chest and returned with the envelope containing Shelby's wax-encrusted journal. "Here you are, Captain," he said, before slumping back into his chair.

"Are you alright, Colonel?" Shelby asked.

Varick sniffed. "General Gates has made me deputy commissioner-general of musters. It is now my job to navigate

138

the elaborate reporting system set up by none other than Gates himself at the beginning of the war when he was Adjutant General. I have to account for the number of officers and men we have here. It is a near impossible task! More men arrive every moment. Gates sent a letter of protest to General Burgoyne over the incident you're up here investigating. It was reprinted in New England papers and now we are flooded with volunteers. And after Stark's victory at Bennington, men are pouring in from the Hampshire Grants, too." The inflection in his voice suggested that these droves of new troops were an undesirable event, but of course both Shelby and Fox knew that he welcomed the added men, just not the duty of counting and organizing them.

"Stark's victory?" Fox chimed in, recalling the marching Hessians he spied while at Fort Edward.

"Oh, haven't you heard?" Burgoyne sent a detachment of Hessians out to forage for food and horses and General Stark's militia routed not only the foraging party, but also a second column of Germans sent out as support. Stark killed near a thousand of those mercenaries, and perhaps just as importantly, Burgoyne's army reaped no supplies for the effort! Now with St. Leger's evacuation, the noose is tightening upon 'Gentlemen Johnny!'" he said elatedly, referring to Burgoyne by his nickname.

Fox smiled at the news of his old comrade's success but his grin faded and he rubbed his chin thoughtfully. "Gates sent a letter blaming Burgoyne for the McCrea slaying, eh?"

"Yes. He did so before I could report your mission to him. He sent word through his aides of my new position and it was several days before I could get an audience with his highness," he mocked.

"Do you think his actions ruinous?" Shelby asked Fox.

The investigator shrugged. "Publicizing the murder has brought more men to this army, as we suspected it would. That

139

is certainly a good thing for Gates as regards the pending fight with Burgoyne. Whether it will have positive or negative long term effects likely depends on whether his accusations prove accurate in the end."

"Assuming there *is* an upcoming fight," Varick interjected sarcastically. "Granny Gates is never one to attack. He is a staunch believer in defensive tactics and unless Burgoyne decides to advance, our opportunity may be squandered. When Arnold returns, I estimate that we will have near ten thousand men here to Burgoyne's seven thousand."

"Let us hope that we take advantage of the situation," Shelby returned optimistically.

"General Schuyler made all of the difficult decisions," Varick said bitterly, "and was proven correct in each circumstance. Were he still in command there would be no question; the British would taste our lead. Gates has been handed a tremendous opportunity. I wonder which will prove superior; his compulsion for the defensive or his desire for glory. Oh, don't think me unprofessional, gentlemen," he said, reading Shelby's expression. "I am only conveying to you what I see quite clearly: Gates is a schemer. He left for Baltimore before the attack at Trenton in order to cajole his political friends in Congress rather than fight. The only reason he has command here is due to his manipulative ways. But do not think command of the Northern Department is his ultimate goal. No, this is a stop-over in his plan to supplant General Washington as commander-in-chief."

Shelby had heard all of the aforementioned criticisms of Gates before; the pejorative of "Granny Gates," that he was much more of a political strategist than a military one, that he had designs on Washington's command... but he also knew that he was one of the most experienced soldiers in their army— he and Charles Lee were the only Patriot officers who had served as regulars in the British army. And Washington had trusted him

140

enough to recommend to Congress that he be given a commission and assigned him the extremely important job of organizing the fledgling army. He was a top notch administrator to be sure, but he had little field experience and Shelby hoped that the criticism that he was obsessively cautious would prove untrue.

Shelby turned to Fox, "Should we try to see General Gates?"

"I will still act as your liaison if you would like," Varick interjected. "I know that he wants updates on all this," he waved his hand frustratingly over the table of records. "So I should be able to get in to see him rather easily now."

Mr. Fox pondered. "I am sure that he is quite busy and if Colonel Varick already apprised him of our mission, I see no real reason to meet with him at this point."

Varick looked disappointed at missing an opportunity to get away from the mundane tasks of commissioner of musters.

"However," Fox followed up, "Colonel, if you have the opportunity to meet with him, you might emphasize that we still do not know the truth about Miss McCrea and that I suggest that it would be best if he suppressed any further comment upon the issue until we have concluded our investigation."

"I am fairly certain that he reached that conclusion after I explained your mission to him, but I will enjoy reminding him." Varick smiled at the chance to dictate instructions to Gates.

"Colonel," Shelby's somber tone caused Varick's grin to evaporate. "I have to report that we lost a member of our party upon our return from Fort Stanwix."

"Oh?" the concern in Varick's voice was readily apparent.

"Yes, if you recall, I left here with a friend, Captain John Rawlings. Today he was felled by a sniper about five miles up the Mohawk. Mr. Fox and I were able to kill the offender, and we buried John— I mean Captain Rawlings. But the commanding officer of his unit should be notified."

The colonel nodded grimly. "He was just up from the highlands, correct?" he asked, paging through his ledgers.

"Yes, that's correct, sir."

"I'll see to it," he replied, in a businesslike tone that did not lack sympathy. "Your things are waiting for you in the same tent you occupied at Stillwater. You'll find it about a hundred yards in that direction." He pointed with the end of his quill as he continued to search his volumes for the deceased's name. The distain Varick felt for his new job in no way diminished his dedication to duty and he lost himself in his task as the pair of investigators slipped from the tent.

Fox and Shelby donated Rawlings's horse to the war effort, turning it over to the quartermaster along with its saddle, which although less than enviable in quality, would not be unwelcome to some ill-equipped officer. However Shelby kept his friend's carbine rifle both as a token of remembrance and also out of practicality. He had left his own musket back in New Jersey but his several brushes with death had left him feeling his dragoon pistols insufficient protection.

The pair found their tent without difficulty. Mr. Fox retrieved his beloved broad brimmed hat, and although he kept the buckskin outfit for possible future use, he longingly returned to the softer fabric of his linen shirt and dark pantaloons. He of course retained his personal deerskin boots which although practical due to the silence, had long ago won his affection out of sheer comfort.

As Mr. Fox was making his transformation, Shelby sat on a cot and cracked open the sealed pages of his journal. He meticulously read through his notes, scanning for any detail he may have omitted from his report back at Fort Dayton.

"Anything else I should know?" Fox asked as he folded the trapper clothing and laid the articles in a corner of the tent.

Shelby shook his head. "Not that I can see. No, I think I gave you a pretty clear account back at Dayton."

142

"Good enough. Let's see if we can rustle up some of those people you interviewed and follow up on that old man facet."

"I'll go ask Colonel Varick if he can provide us with some assistance. He should at least know where we can find them."

Varick was only too happy to take a break from his books and with the help of a few enlisted men, rounded up all of the individuals with whom Shelby had spoken, with the exception of Mrs. Braithwaite, the washerwoman, who could not be found and two of the militiamen who were out on patrol.

Mr. Fox assumed the role of interrogator and posed simple and direct questions in the attempt to ascertain the identity of the elderly, stooped man alleged to have had meetings with Jane McCrea. The inquiry proved fruitless until the husband and wife, Otto and Sarah Jacobs, sparked a ray of hope.

"What about that Mr... Mr. Burrows?" Sarah asked her husband after the name finally registered in her brain.

Shelby and Fox looked at each other expectantly.

"Mr. Burrows?" Fox asked, coaxing Otto to continue the thought.

The man squinted as if he were considering if the man truly did fit the profile. "Yes... Yes, I suppose it could be Mr. Burrows."

"Who is this Mr. Burrows?" Shelby broke in impatiently.

"He's not really from Fort Edward. He's a farmer from further north. I *think* his Christian name is Jeffery, but I'm not certain. He hails from somewhere north of Sandy Hill, I think." He scratched his head as if trying to confirm the notion by retrieving it from a recess of his mind. Finally he gave up and continued. "Anyway, a couple of times a year he floats a shipment of his crops down the Hudson and then travels on horseback back up the military road through Fort Edward on his return trip."

A sour expression screwed over Shelby's face. "Are you sure he fits the description? That sounds like an arduous journey for an old man."

Otto Jacobs laughed. "Well I can't rightly say, but it's the closest I can come to the man you're looking for. He hires the boat, so he's not actually doing the work getting the crops down the river. I don't know him well at all. I only spoke with him on one occasion. But he is in his early sixties, about six feet in height, or would be, except for the fact that he is stooped over."

"Did he and Miss McCrea know one another?" Mr. Fox asked.

"That I cannot say," Otto looked to his wife who shrugged her shoulders. "Neither John nor Jane ever mentioned him."

Shelby thought to himself, "That does not discount the connection, if they were both spies."

"And you say his place is north of Fort Edward?" the captain asked in a disappointed tone knowing that travelling that far behind the British lines would be extremely difficult if not impossible.

"His *place* is. But *he* isn't. I heard that he fled south to stay with relatives."

The gloom vanished from Shelby's features.

"Do you know where we might find him?" Mr. Fox interjected.

"No." The man shook his head.

"General Schuyler would know," Sarah Jacobs interjected. "He knows practically everyone in the region."

When nothing further could be learned, they dismissed the couple, thanking them for their cooperation.

"So, where do we go from here?" Shelby asked, closing his notebook upon his pencil.

"Albany, I expect." Fox replied. "I believe General Schuyler is there preparing his defense before he appears before Congress.

144

Hopefully he will be able to tell us where to find this Mr. Burrows."

Chapter 14

The investigators headed south the following morning, taking the well-travelled river road that paralleled the west bank of the Hudson. The morning air was warm, but August was waning and the mist that lingered above the river served as a premonition of autumn's approach.

They were passed by numerous bands of men headed in the opposite direction, eager to join the force now commanded by Horatio Gates. The army had been swelling since the end of July, but up until now the recruits had worn solemn expressions and been motivated primarily by the fear of Indians overrunning their homesteads and slaughtering their loved ones. The faces of the men they encountered on the river road however bore prideful smiles and expressions of glowing optimism. Word of Stark's victory at Bennington and St. Leger's retreat from Fort Stanwix had spread like wildfire and the result on the populace had been electric. Rumor was that Gates was about to move back to Stillwater, and perhaps even further north. If this were so, the army of the Northern Department would be heading *toward* the British for the first time since the disastrous Canadian expedition.

Although the investigators did not push their horses, they still covered the twelve miles from the Sprouts down to Albany in less than three hours.

Albany was the prize Burgoyne was really after. The city was the most important in New York aside from New York City itself, and if the British could conquer it, it was likely they could drive a wedge in the rebellion by separating New England from the rest of the renegade colonies.

Even though there were a fair amount of Tories in New York State, Albany itself had sided stanchly with the Patriots. The city had been the site of the first gathering of colonial representatives back in 1754 where Benjamin Franklin had proposed the Albany Plan of Union-- the first conception of politically joining the colonies together. Although the plan was rejected, that assemblage set the stage for the later Continental Congresses. With the outbreak of revolutionary violence in Massachusetts in 1775, Patriots seized control of the city's government and made it the seat of the cause in the region.

Although the city had been in English hands for more than a hundred years, it still maintained much of its original Dutch flavor. The waterfront teemed with activity, and Shelby thought that it looked much like the harbor at Baltimore with its numerous wharves and busy landings. The pair negotiated the bustling streets and approached the three story brick city hall, still known by the Dutch translation *Stadt Huys*. It was the largest building in the city after the Dutch Reform Church and the remnants of Fort Albany, which at present was serving as a prison for captured Loyalists.

"Should I inquire where we might find General Schuyler?" Shelby asked his companion.

"No. He will be at his mansion. It is on the southeast side of town. I know how to get there."

Mr. Fox led the way south, crossing the Beaverkill, a stream that cut through the city on its inevitable convergence with the mighty Hudson.

"Schuyler's land begins here," Fox informed just after they had traversed the stream. "He calls his spread *The Pastures*. It is about eighty acres, I would say."

As they approached the house, it confirmed that Philip Schuyler was indeed one of the wealthiest men in the region. The large brick home resided upon a knoll, dominating its surroundings. The giant square mansion appeared to have two

147

floors but the presence of dormers atop the house betrayed a third one as well. The home had been designed by Schuyler himself although most of the construction had taken place while he was away in England almost twenty years earlier.

"That is some house," Shelby muttered.

"Don't forget he has a country one as well," Fox replied to the rhetorical comment. "And about twenty thousand acres in the Saratoga region."

A young black boy came running around the side of the house. The smiling youth asked if he should attend to their horses, and they gratefully handed him their reins so that he might lead their mounts off to the stables.

"Here you are, son," Fox said, pushing a coin into the youth's palm.

The boy shook his head. "Oh no, sir. The Gen'ral wouldn't like that."

The Quaker smiled reassuringly and placed an affectionate hand upon the boy's shoulder. "I know that General Schuyler might not approve, thinking it inhospitable for his guests to pay for services he offers as a courteous host. But I am not compensating you for stabling our horses; I am providing you a gratuity for doing such a good job of it."

The confused expression that clouded over the boy's face demonstrated that some of Mr. Fox's vocabulary was beyond his comprehension, so the investigator followed with a simpler explanation. "The silver is a *gift* for giving our horses the best treatment possible. I will make sure the general understands."

At this reassurance the youth's lips parted in a smile and he accepted the coin, promising to treat their mounts with the greatest care.

Another servant met them at the front door. He was likewise black, but a few years older and wore the fine clothing of a house attendant. The man did not seem surprised to find two armed men upon the doorstep. Perhaps Captain Shelby's uniform

148

assured him that they were at least friendly. When they introduced themselves and asked if the general could meet with them briefly, the man disappeared. Captain Shelby's eyes roved toward his companion, curious if his disdain for slavery would show through. However the Quaker waited patiently, his self-possession mastering the contempt he held for the institution and those who chose to sustain it.

A few minutes later the man returned and showed them into a large library where the general was at work behind a desk. At a nearby table a bookish looking fellow was sifting through piles of papers.

"Come in," Schuyler called from across the room. "Have a seat," he said, offering the chairs opposite his impressive mahogany desk.

Before proceeding over to the general the men walked to a corner near the doorway. They propped their rifles against the wall and Shelby removed his baldrick, hanging his sword over the back of a nearby chair before pulling his pistols from his belt and placing them upon the seat. The men's powder horns and cartridge boxes were likewise slung over the chair. The officer's comrade slid the tomahawk from the small of his back and rested it atop the captain's guns. However, Shelby noticed that he did not unsheathe his large hunting knife. Whether this was an oversight or a habitual precaution against defenselessness, the captain could not say.

"I didn't expect to see you two," Schuyler stated, somewhat dispassionately after they had taken their seats. It was obvious that his mind was dominated by pressing issues. "Can I offer you a drink?" He rubbed the bridge of his nose wearily. "Some brandy?" And then looking at Mr. Fox he quickly added, "Tea perhaps?"

"Two cups of tea would be fine," Shelby answered for both. "Thank you."

149

Schuyler waved an order to the servant waiting in the doorway and then turned to the clerk at the table, "Jenkins, take a break while I meet with these gentlemen." The man bowed slightly and without a word left the room.

"I'm busy preparing my case. I insisted that they court martial me," Schuyler informed. "Sam Adams and John Hancock have got Congress believing that Ticonderoga's loss was my doing. I wasn't even in command there, it was St. Clair," he grumbled. "Anyway, I'm not about to have my reputation sullied just because those New Englanders wanted to hijack the Northern Department for their crony Gates. With the trial, I'll have my say, and they'll have to listen."

"Your plan to relieve Fort Stanwix was a stunning success," Shelby said, hoping to lubricate their relationship with the general; knowing that Mr. Fox would never make such an obsequious overture.

"Yes, well it was not without risk," he warmed a bit. "But I felt it necessary. If we faced Burgoyne to the north *and* St. Leger to the west, I don't know if we could have held Albany. I only hope that Gates doesn't squander what we've accomplished," he brooded. "He doesn't seem too inclined to act. He doesn't know the first thing about the area, and isn't overly anxious to educate himself," he sniffed. "Do you know that when I graciously offered my services in apprising him of the topography, he chose to not even include me in his council of war? He had every other general there but me."

Despite Gates' political differences with Schuyler, to Shelby this petty maneuver seemed pure folly. He shook his head likening it to cutting off one's nose to spite the face.

Just then the servant arrived with their tea, and General Schuyler roused from his indignation. "So what brings you two here, may I ask? More on that McCrea affair, I suppose?" he said, a milder tone in his voice.

150

Mr. Fox spoke for the first time. Whether he had been brooding over communing with a slave owner, or merely practicing his patient stoicism, Shelby could only guess. "Yes. We are still investigating the matter and we are interested in interviewing a gentleman named Jeffrey Burrows. We were told that you might know him."

"Burrows?" Schuyler tapped his forefinger upon his temple. After a few seconds he said, 'Yes. Yes, I know the man. He's a farmer. Owns maybe a hundred acres about fifteen miles north of Fort Edward. In the past he's hired one of my sloops to bring his crops down the Hudson. What about him?"

"We would like to speak with him," Fox reiterated. "It is rumored that he fled south to stay with relatives and that you might know where we could find him."

Schuyler scratched his chin. "Bartholomew!" he called out.

"Yes, sir?" the house slave asked, appearing in the doorway.

"Paul Dekker, the tanner. Didn't he marry Jeffrey Burrows' daughter?"

"Yes sir, I believe that he did."

"I thought so," Schuyler said to himself. "His tannery is over in Ricketts' Glenn, isn't it?" he called back to the slave.

"Yes sir."

"Alright, thank you Bartholomew," he said, dismissing the servant. He turned back to the pair of investigators. "I would try there. Ricketts' Glenn is across the river about twenty miles southeast of here."

"We were well advised to speak with you," Shelby again placated the general.

Schuyler turned to look at a handsome clock that sat upon the fireplace mantel. "Gentlemen, we will be having luncheon in just a quarter hour. Would you do me the honor of dining with us?"

Captain Shelby was thankful not only for the offer but that he had taken the opportunity to mollify the beleaguered

151

aristocrat, thinking his flattery may have played a part in the invitation. He looked to his partner for an answer.

"That would be fine," Mr. Fox said in an even tone. "However, first I want to make sure that you will not be cross with the lad who took our horses. Out of loyalty to you, he tried to turn down the coin I gave him. But I insisted that he take it." Shelby cringed slightly at the sternness in his partner's voice, hoping that he had not just sentenced them to eating the hard biscuits they had packed from the Sprouts encampment.

"What's that?" Schuyler asked distractedly as he had already returned to examining the papers upon his desk. "Oh. That is alright. Although I must say you're less frugal than other Quakers I've known," he laughed.

As with most important men, hospitality was as much a matter of honor as justifying his military record. During the luncheon the general was polite and accommodating although his mind could not wander far from the bitterness he felt for Gates and the New Englanders who had schemed for his removal. The general's wife dined with them as well, and was a congenial hostess, but she was obviously disturbed by the offense done her husband and had no compunctions about voicing these opinions. Mrs. Schuyler was still an attractive woman at forty-three despite giving birth a half-dozen times. And her hostile undercurrents did not prevent her from proving somewhat enjoyable company. The younger children were sequestered from the adults during the meal so that they might not be alarmed by talk of the war or the upcoming court martial and the older ones were absent, exploring their own endeavors.

By afternoon the investigators were preparing to leave when it was noticed that Shelby's horse had thrown a shoe. Schuyler had one of his servants take the beast to a blacksmith in town but by the time the matter was rectified, the pair would never be in time to make the ferry before it ceased operation for the day. The gracious general insisted that they spend the night and not begin their trek until the next morning.

After a sumptuous dinner consisting of more courses than seemed practical, Mr. Fox retired to their room. His scholarly inclinations had been stifled by their adventurous activities and he longed for a quiet corner in which to return to the siege of Troy. Captain Shelby however spent the evening in the company of General and Mrs. Schuyler and their older children. It was the family's habit to occupy the twilight hours in the large parlor, engaged in conversation or reading either privately or aloud to one another. The general's secretary had dined with them but that was his sole respite as he returned to the library and the preparation of Schuyler's case.

"That Mr. Fox is an odd sort," Mrs. Schuyler commented, as Bartholomew, the house servant, poured some claret into her glass.

"Quaker," her husband stated curtly. "They're a peculiar lot. Not an altogether bad one though," he said, lighting his pipe. "General Greene is saying that the fix Burgoyne is finding himself in is my doing," he said, his admiration for Greene obviously enhanced by the general's commendation of his efforts.

"That should carry weight," Shelby replied, waving off Bartholomew's offer of a pipe. "General Washington holds Greene in high regard."

"That's true," he paused to emit a puff of smoke. "But Washington is answerable to Congress and they are the ones who removed me, not General Washington."

"So this Mr. Fox just hides himself away?" Mrs. Schuyler returned to her original thought as if offended by the man's absence.

Despite the fondness Shelby had established for his partner, he did find his quirks irregular and could not endorse his

153

aloofness. The most he could bring himself to do was to attempt to soften the perception of Fox's eccentricities.

"I have only known him a short time but he has proven to be brave, compassionate and tenacious. But he is an enigma," laughed Shelby. "I believe that he prefers solitude and is only pulled out of his self-imposed isolation when his dedication to stronger principles necessitate it."

"Don't his principles require he disassociate himself from warfare?" the lady inquired. The hostility had left her voice and she appeared to be growing as intrigued about the singular Mr. Fox as Shelby had become.

The captain took a sip of brandy before answering. "As I said, I have only known him a short while and I suspect that even if we had been friends for years, it would be difficult to understand him completely. However, I have found that he believes strongly in the tenets of his religion but also in those of the Revolution. It seems to me that when the two come into conflict his personal ethos forces him to begrudgingly side with the latter."

"And what of you, Captain? You are a bit of an enigma yourself," Schuyler said with a twinkle in his eye. "If I am not mistaken, your father is hardly an ardent Patriot."

Shelby's face flushed. The crimson hue was not the result of embarrassment, but from a visceral response of general resentment the mention of his father brought. "You know my father, sir?"

"No, not directly. But before I was commissioned, I was a member of Congress." A cloud of blue smoke escaped his mouth and drifted in front of his face. "And I recall a delegate from Maryland, William Paca, tried to enlist your father in the cause. He was quite frustrated that your father remained equivocal on the subject."

"I assure you sir, that I do not share his ambivalence." Shelby's reply may have been colored with umbrage but the hard tone of his voice and the expansion of his chest gave more of an impression of pride in his own commitment to the Revolution.

"I have no doubt of that," the general smiled reassuringly, perhaps a bit apologetic at his dig. "A letter followed you to Stillwater from General Alexander, mentioning your courage in Long Island and New Jersey."

The statement did indeed mollify Shelby and the discussion turned to the more pleasant topics of literature and particularly of certain Shakespearian plays, a number of which the general had the privilege of seeing performed in the country of their origin during his time in London two decades earlier.

When Captain Shelby crept into the bedchamber, the gentle rhythm of Mr. Fox's breathing indicated that he had abandoned Agamemnon and his army sometime earlier. The young man disrobed and slipped into his own bed as quietly as possible. He reached over to the end table and extinguished the candle he had carried into the room with him and rolled over, grateful for the soothing comfort of the expensive goose-down mattress. Yet, despite the unparalleled succor of the luxurious bed, he had difficulty falling asleep. The image of his father kept drifting through his mind. He glanced over at his slumbering partner, wondering if he held some secret method for attaining peace of mind in spite of recurring demons.

Chapter 15

The next morning dawned with a dewy crispness which confirmed that the calendar page had turned from the eighth to the ninth month of the year. Bartholomew offered the men a hearty breakfast, which they readily accepted. However, they dined alone as Mrs. Schuyler and the children had yet to awaken and the master of the house had risen even earlier than the investigators to attend to some business outside of the home before returning to the preparation for his court martial.

"Your horses are waiting out front," the house servant informed as he removed their empty plates.

"Thank you, sir," Mr. Fox stated as he extended his hand.

A perplexed expression fell over the slave's face either due to being called "sir" or at the unexpected offering of the white man's hand. He put one of the plates down on the tabletop and clumsily shook the Quaker's hand.

"It was nice of you to see that we had something to eat before we left," Fox said.

"Umm, that's… that's alright, sir," he replied awkwardly.

Shelby watched this exchange with both curiosity and humor. He suppressed a chuckle at the slave's puzzled manner but he also focused on his partner. At first he believed that Mr. Fox was trying to make an overt point to the house servant about the inequities of slavery. But in reading the man's face, he saw no sermonizing in his blue-gray eyes. "No," he thought, "his behavior is effortless. He is merely paying Bartholomew the courtesy he would pay any man who has done him a good turn."

"Please tell the general that we thank him for his help and his hospitality," Shelby added as they reached the front door.

"I will, sir," he replied as the pair re-armed themselves, pulling on their rifles and adorning their various other weapons as well. "And you have a safe journey, now."

Shelby thought that he sensed a touch of sentimentality in the last statement uncharacteristic in the formal demeanor of the valet and he wondered if his friend had elicited it through his simple, if unusual, profession of gratitude.

As the door closed behind them they found themselves face to face with the youth they had first met upon reaching the Schuyler mansion. He stood grinning as he held their reins at the ready.

"Ah, thank you m' lad," Fox said with a pat on his shoulder as he climbed into the saddle.

"I took good care of 'em!" he smiled up at the man in the broad-brimmed black hat.

"I knew that you would," Fox returned. "And I spoke with General Schuyler, as I said that I would. He has no problem with the gratuity I gave you."

"Thank you, sir!" he returned. Whether he now understood the term or not, it was apparent that he comprehended the greater meaning that his master would not be angry with him.

"Good day to you young man," Fox stated, tipping his hat and winking before he and Captain Shelby took to the road.

The ferry operating out of Albany would require them to backtrack northward into the center of the city, so they opted to continue south, hiring a boatman further downriver. They again trekked along the road that paralleled the western bank of the Hudson, leaving General Schuyler and Albany behind. The waterway teemed with boat traffic. Sloops, schooners, yawls and barges were but some of the craft Captain Shelby was able to identify jockeying along the glassy surface as they headed to or from the hub of commerce on the Hudson.

Some six miles downstream they approached Schodack Island-- a large, long islet that hugged the Hudson's eastern bank at its northern tip. The river had begun to broaden, and would continue to do so as it carved its way ever closer to the sea. A ferry in operation at the north end of the island provided the shortest, easiest crossing as the boatman utilized the point of the island as part of his operation.

"What is the news, Captain?" the ferryman called congenially as they approached the landing.

"The news is good," Shelby smiled back. "St. Leger is in full retreat from Fort Stanwix and the Hessians were defeated in the Hampshire Grants by General Stark."

"So it's true, eh?" The man lifted his flaccid black hat with one hand and scratched his head with the other. "We'd heard talk as such. Rumors run at a sprint while the facts are still getting their boots on," he laughed. "Glad to hear that it's true. I can put up your horses on this side if you'd like, or will you be taking them with you?"

"No, we'll be taking them," Shelby announced.

"Alright, I'll use the bigger boat then," he said, climbing from the dock, through a dory, to a larger barge.

"What is the fare?" the Quaker chimed in. When the man named a price, Mr. Fox frowned and leaned over to whisper something in his partner's ear.

"Alright," the ferryman called out with a laugh. I can see that you're Patriots, as am I, so I'll give you the discount rate." He named a price marginally lower, but this small reduction satisfied Mr. Fox's frugal sensibilities.

"Thaddeus!" the man yelled toward a small shack some distance away.

"Yes, Pa?" a dark-haired teenage boy called back, stepping around the side of the building.

"Get your brother. We need to take these gentlemen over!"

With a nod of his head the teen disappeared. A minute later he reemerged, an exact duplicate of the boy walking at his side. Shelby nearly rubbed his eyes to make sure he was not suffering a stroke of the sun, but he quickly realized that the brothers were twins. The clones climbed aboard the ferry and readied the craft in an unspoken unison that either betrayed long experience or some inaudible method of communication shared by the replica brothers. The riders dismounted and then when the ramp was lowered, walked their mounts aboard. The ramp was put back in place and in a matter of minutes the family of boatmen was hauling on the thick rope that dragged the vessel back and forth across the river. On the western side of the Hudson, this cable made several turns around a stout oak and was anchored at the other side around a sister tree that resided at the end of Schodack Island.

They boys said not a word during the crossing, and even their loquacious father confined his verbiage to directing his sons in their job. In less than fifteen minutes the investigative team found themselves exiting the ferry at the northern extremity of the island. They remounted and forded the shallows separating the point of Schodack from the mainland before continuing south along the eastern bank.

The travelers went without a midday meal but in the evening found an inn that not only offered a fair dinner of broiled shad, but also provided them lodging for the evening. The keeper of the establishment was a beady-eyed, bald headed, elf of a man whose personality could best be described through the simile of the color gray. He was neither gregarious nor rude and although ready enough to take their money, he did not appear anxious to win any return business. Shelby figured him for one of the lot totally disinterested in the war from any and all perspectives.

159

The following morning found the two again upon the road, although they had turned eastward as per the directions they had received from the gnomish inn keeper.

"Excuse me," Shelby called to two boys coming up the wagon ruts that served as a thoroughfare in the rural vicinity.

"Yes sir?" one of the youths answered.

"Can you direct us to Ricketts Glenn?"

The boys appeared to be in the range of ten or twelve years and were carrying fishing poles. Fox and Shelby had left the banks of the Hudson several hours before so the captain figured that the lads must be headed to try their luck at some nearby stream or pond.

"Sure," the other boy replied, turning an admiringly jealous eye toward the soldier's sword. "Keep headed the way you're going. In a little while you'll reach a big willow. The road forks off there. Stay to the right and you'll be in Ricketts Glenn before too long."

Shelby forgave the youth's imprecise judge of distance and time, glad that they were not exceedingly far from their destination. "Thank you," he replied, giving the pair a salute, which they excitedly returned, surprised and elated by the gesture.

After another mile Captain Shelby broke the long silence that had descended over the riders, "So, if this Burrows is indeed our man, do you suspect him to be a British spy or one of our own?"

Mr. Fox shrugged his shoulders. "He fled Burgoyne's forces... but of course that might be a ruse. It is exactly what one might expect from a Loyalist agent in order to maintain his cover."

"Would it not have been beneficial to him to remain behind the British lines if he was a spy for our side?" Shelby queried.

"I would suspect yes, unless he was found out, or in danger of being found out."

"So his flight southward may not have been from fear of Burgoyne's Indians but to avoid being hanged as a spy," Shelby considered.

"It is plausible. However, remember, if he is our man, he could just as easily be working for the enemy."

"That's right," Shelby pondered aloud, "We don't know whether Miss McCrea was partial to her brother's cause or that of her fiancé."

The town of Ricketts Glenn was situated along a lake not far from the Massachusetts border. "Town" was perhaps an overstatement as there were no more than two dozen structures in the little settlement. As Fox and Shelby approached, they noticed that most of the buildings were clustered at the near end of the village. The first structure was a handsome little clapboard-sided barn with wagon wheels of various sizes leaning against the outside wall. An adolescent boy gave them a friendly nod as he rolled out another wheel and began fitting it to a buckboard that was short one of its own. A modest wooden sign reading "Wheelwright" creaked in the gentle breeze as they passed.

A blacksmith's shop stood next to the wheelwright, and although the craftsman remained unseen, the heavy clank of his hammer betrayed that he was plying his vocation somewhere nearby. They passed a number of other shops intermingled with simple, but attractive houses. Beyond this strand the sound of running water met their ears. Presently they ascertained the reason; a lake had been created by the construction of a dam. A bridge crossed over the spillway where the body of water morphed back into a small river. Here a saw mill made use of the weight of the water as it fell from the spillway. An overshot wheel caught the liquid as it poured down, driving the mechanisms within the mill to power the saw blades.

Further downstream an undershot wheel harnessed the power of the flowing river to grind grain in a grist mill. The last of the enterprises that lined the river was the tannery. It was a stone structure with large, open barn doors. The place had been situated furthest downstream so that its noxious wastes would flush beyond the town.

Large barrels filled with oak bark sat outside the building, waiting to be ground into the coarse powder in which the hides would be soaked so that the tannin in the bark could pull the moisture from the hides, in effect turning them into leather.

Shelby and Fox dismounted, wrapping their reins around the top rail of a fence that ran from the front of the tannery around the side of the building and back to the tan yard. They peered around curiously as no human could be seen.

"Hello!" Captain Shelby called out. When no answer came, Mr. Fox waved his hand, beckoning his partner to follow him into the recesses of the barn-like structure. Inside they passed piles of hides and vats containing the brown liquid in which still more hides soaked. "Hello?" Shelby called again as they moved through the shadowy interior. The only response however was the sound of a whispery crackle from somewhere deeper within the building.

Mr. Fox again waved his companion onward and when they reached a planked wooden door, he knocked. The door was set into a wooden wall that seemed to partition the building in half. Receiving no answer, he pushed it open and slid through the opening. Beyond the door they found the source of the noise. A lonely ox tethered to the end of a long pole, somberly walked in an endless circle. The other end of the pole was affixed to a millstone which sat atop a second stone and between which the oak bark was being ground into the powder necessary for the tanner's occupation.

They were now at the rear of the barn where two large doors, identical to those in the front also stood agape, looking out into the rear of the tan yard. Almost immediately a young man

162

pushing a wheel barrow came around the corner, entering the building.

"Oh, hello," he said congenially as he wheeled his load into a corner and dumped its contents of bark, adding to a standing pile. The teenager was lean and hatless and his brown tannin-stained hands were just a shade darker than the hue of his pulled back hair. Coming back over to them he asked, "Can I help you gentlemen?" His manner was carefree and friendly. He was apparently not the least bit phased by the fact that Shelby was in uniform or that both men were heavily armed.

"We are looking for Mr. Dekker. I believe that he is the owner of this establishment?" the captain asked.

"Right you are," he smiled. "Mr. Dekker is up at the shop."

"The shop?" Shelby asked.

Realizing that they were obviously new to town, the apprentice furthered, "It's over in town, opposite the blacksmith. We ship most of our goods down to New York, but the local farmers need things too. We used to sell some of our wares right out of here, but when Mrs. Dekker wanted to open a chandlery, Mr. Dekker made it kind of a dual purpose shop."

"Alright, thank you," Shelby smirked, humored by the somewhat strange union of a candle and leather-goods shop. Mr. Fox echoed his thanks and the pair ambled out to their horses and trotted back into town.

The reverberating metallic clanging from the blacksmith shop grew louder as they retraced their path. "Here it is," Captain Shelby said, dismounting.

The aromas of scented wax and tooled leather made an odd combination as they stepped inside the quaint little storefront. "Can I be of service gentlemen?" A plain-faced, though courteous woman asked without looking away from the shelf she was stocking.

"Would you be Mrs. Dekker?" Mr. Fox queried.

"That I would," she returned as she continued her task.

163

"And you are the daughter of Jeffrey Burrows?"

"I am," she replied, turning toward them for the first time.

"We were sent here by General Schuyler. We need to speak with your father." Fox said.

A worried look came over her face. "Why?" she asked, her hand frozen in the act of depositing a candle upon the shelf.

"Is he here?" Shelby asked in an assertive tone.

"He's in the back. We live in the back and upstairs."

Just then Mr. Fox leaped across the room to where a curtain cordoned off a doorway. He grabbed through the curtain, pulling a man into the room, violently pinning him face down upon the counter. Fox's left hand held the man's head to the surface while his right gripped the man's wrist behind his back, forcing him to drop the hatchet he had been holding.

Shelby had been startled by his friend's sudden action but quickly recovered and was in the motion of pulling his sword from its scabbard when the woman ran over to him and tried to push the weapon back in place. "Oh! Oh! That's my husband! Don't hurt him, please!"

"I wasn't up to nothing!" Paul Dekker spat out the side of his mouth. "I was just making sure you wasn't rough with my wife is all!" he barked with some difficulty, his nose still pressed hard against the countertop.

Fox released the man, and as the tanner stood rubbing his neck, the Quaker sized him up through narrowed eyes. "Alright," he said finally. "But we are not men to be trifled with. We are here on official business for the Continental Army. It is possible that we will be on our way very shortly. The more helpful you are, the faster we can dispense with our business."

"Did you really come from General Schuyler?" Paul Dekker asked.

"Yes," Shelby replied curtly.

"Well, if that's so, we've nothing to fear," the tanner said, although the apprehension in his voice hinted that he was less

164

relieved than he professed and merely trying to placate the invaders. "Come with me, gentlemen. I'll take you to Emmie's father."

Both husband and wife led the way through the curtained threshold that connected to the living quarters beyond the shop. Two small girls rushed past them in a game of tag and a sharp rebuke from their mother to stop running in the house had no effect as the duo carried their game up the narrow staircase that ran to one side of the hallway.

The investigators followed Mr. and Mrs. Dekker past a parlor into a kitchen at the rear of the house. There, behind the table sat a graying, bearded man. Although seated, they could easily recognize the curve of his upper back that showed his less than ideal posture. He puffed on a long-stemmed briar pipe and was absorbed in a book; the distance at which he held from his face suggested that he could benefit from a pair of glasses like the ones used by Mr. Fox.

"Papa?" the woman said uneasily as they came into the room.

"Eh?" he asked without removing the pipe-stem from his teeth or looking up.

"These men want to see you."

"They do, do they?" he said, shifting his eyes off of his reading and scrutinizing the investigators. "Have a seat," he said, pointing to vacant chairs with the stem of his pipe. The older man did not seem nervous, or even curious as he closed the book on his finger. "Get us some coffee, will you, Emmie," he directed before returning his pipe to his mouth.

Mr. Fox and Captain Shelby accepted the beverage and then Mr. Fox turned to the couple who stood nervously in the doorway. "We would like to converse with Mr. Burrows privately."

Mr. and Mrs. Dekker grudgingly melted back down the hallway. When Shelby and Fox turned back to the elderly man, he eyed them with a casual coolness. "You boys seem to know who I am. Might I ask who you might be?"

"I am Captain Shelby and this is Mr. Fox," the officer returned with an equally unruffled manner. "We were sent up to Stillwater to investigate the death of Miss Jane McCrea and were told that you made trips through Fort Edward and might have known the girl."

"Sure, I've been through Fort Edward a lot," he said, adjusting himself in his seat. "Dirty business, that murder."

Shelby was unsure if the old man had purposely avoided answering the second part of his query. He asked again, "And did you know the girl?"

Mr. Burrows took a few contemplative draws on his pipe. "Yes. I knew her."

Shelby's back stiffened.

"She was sister of the local militia colonel, right?" Burrows added.

"Of course," Shelby returned impatiently. "What was the nature of your relationship?" he asked sternly.

"Relationship?" He laughed. "What relationship? I said I knew her. That is, I knew who she was."

"So you did not know her intimately?" Shelby's mouth hung open in disappointment.

"Never spoke a word to her in my life," he returned from the corner of his mouth without removing his pipe.

The captain's muscles tightened again as he recovered from his initial disappointment and realized that despite the man's relaxed manner, he might be lying. He was about to assert himself more aggressively when his partner jumped in.

"When did you lose the leg?" Mr. Fox calmly asked.

Shelby started at the question.

"Got the injury on the farm in April, sawbones took the leg off in May."

166

"I thought as much," Fox said, as the surprised Captain Shelby inelegantly ducked his head under the table to view the farmer's missing shin and foot. Mr. Fox stood. "Sorry to have troubled you, sir. You are not the man we were looking for." The shocked captain still sat at the table, open-mouthed. The Quaker had to physically tug on his arm to return him to reality.

Chapter 16

The pair of investigators walked back through the curtain and exited the shop, much to the relief of the nervous husband and wife pretending to busy themselves with the chores of the establishment. The men were barely through the door when the couple rushed back to assure themselves that that the patriarch was alright, as well as assuage their curiosity about the peculiar interview.

"How did you know he was missing that leg? Did you see under the table as we walked in?" Shelby asked as he untethered his mount.

Fox's shoulders rocked as he noiselessly laughed. "I could tell by the way he was sitting. After that, I peeked around the room and leaning against the far side of the cupboard was a pair of crutches. You could not see them from your angle."

The captain mimicked his partner and climbed aboard his horse. "Obviously if he lost his leg when he said he did, he could not have been the one meeting with Miss McCrea at the times suggested by the washerwoman. But how do you know he was telling the truth about *when* the appendage was removed? If it were more recent, then he could still be our man."

The crooked smile crossed the Quaker's face. "I have no doubt that had you seen the crutches you would have noticed the worn sheen on the armpits of the man's shirt. No, he has been using those supports for many months."

Shelby exhaled heavily. Aggravated at this latest roadblock, he failed to find humor in his partner's playful explanation.

"So what do we do now?" Shelby asked as they turned their horses toward the roadway.

168

"I suppose we head back to the Sprouts and I will go undercover again behind the lines to see if I can find this 'Le Loup', the Indian who allegedly committed the murder."

As they began trotting back toward the entrance to the town, Shelby pondered his partner's plan and did not find it savory in the least. It is true that he had already carried their investigation to terrain under British control, but that had been different; his task had been to surreptitiously obtain intelligence, not to confront a warrior and forcibly extract information from him. If it were even possible for Mr. Fox to find this Le Loup, he would surely have to do battle with other members of his war party and perhaps even British soldiers as well. Despite Mr. Fox's nonchalance, the stratagem was dangerous in the extreme and the captain did not expect that Fox could accomplish it without being killed or captured. Shelby was about to voice this opinion when he noticed a small crowd had gathered ahead near the shade of a large maple tree. The gathering likewise drew Mr. Fox's attention and when they saw two girls hurrying to reach the spot, Captain Shelby could not help but ask, "Excuse me Miss, but what is the cause of the excitement?"

"Harvey Birch has just arrived!" one of the young teens blurted.

"Harvey Birch?" the captain repeated questioningly.

"The peddler, Harvey Birch," she panted with some exasperation.

"A peddler?" Shelby pressed. "But you have shops here in town."

The girl snorted. "We can get these homespun things any time," she waved her hand dismissively toward the town. "Harvey Birch brings things from Manhattan, Albany, even Boston sometimes. He even has imported goods!"

As Fox and Shelby neared the gathering, they found a dozen people, mostly women and girls, surrounding a lanky man encumbered with a large, heavy pack. The peddler's face was

169

obscured by the wide brim of his droopy brown hat, but his mannerisms suggested a friendly nature and pleasant disposition. The travelling merchant was being barraged with questions regarding his latest stock and was doing his best to calm the crowd, promising to display all he had with him. Just as the investigators were passing, the peddler struggled out from under his massive load, depositing the lumbering, ponderous pack, upon the ground. As he did so, Shelby noticed that despite relieving the weight, he did not straighten to his full six feet in height. Rather, he stayed slightly bent as the constant burden had obviously effected an erosion of his posture.

The significance of the sight hit both Captain Shelby and Mr. Fox at the same instant and even the unflappable Quaker's face bore an expression of surprised revelation. The look they gave one another communicated their thoughts without need of verbiage. Fox dismounted and his partner followed this lead. Shelby was a bit surprised that Fox had not led them off to some cover and waited for the crowd to disperse before proceeding, but his swift and decisive maneuver seemed to confirm the investigator's certainty.

The peddler was in a congenial exchange with several ladies, touting the quality of a bolt of lace when they walked up behind him. Fox, in a decidedly unQuaker-like tactic, gripped the back of the man's collar and hauled him backwards, away from the group. "We need a minute of your time, sir," he said, his urbane and mannerly voice in direct contrast to the brutality of his actions.

"What? What is this all about?" one of the startled ladies shrieked.

"Unhand him, you!" another bellowed.

"Let him alone there, feller," one of the few men in the group moved forward, daring to assert himself.

Shelby aggressively slid into the space vacated by the peddler, a menacing hand upon his sword, the other upon one of his pistols. The antagonistic man stepped back.

"We are on official business. You may wait here, or you may leave. But do not interfere." The captain's comportment and tone stung of authority and a hush fell over the group.

With deliberate strides, Shelby caught up with his partner, who was still dragging the peddler backward. When he had pulled the man some twenty feet away, he released his grip. The travelling merchant grabbed at his throat, the front of his collar having caused him a small amount of asphyxiation during the encounter. Mr. Fox spun him around in a rather violent fashion but when his eyes fell on the face of the man, his grim, furrowed brow melted into an expression of astonishment. He stood looking at Harvey Birch's face for a frozen moment, neither man uttering a word. Finally, he patted the man on the shoulder and turned to the perplexed captain.

"Come on," he said curtly, and then abruptly walked back to his horse and climbed into the saddle. The mystified officer looked at the peddler, and then back at his partner before hurrying to his own mount to avoid being left as Mr. Fox had already begun to ride out of town.

*   *   *

They were a quarter mile outside of Ricketts Glenn before the flabbergasted officer could summon his voice. "Do you mind telling me what that was all about?" he asked incredulously. Unfortunately for the exasperated solider, the Quaker did not reply, his pensive expression showed that he was deep in thought. However, Shelby would not be dissuaded. "I take it that he was not our man either," he said in a sarcastic tone as much a result of the frustration of their quest as his confusion over his partner's actions. Still the investigator remained silent.

171

Shelby was simply too befuddled and aggravated to let the matter rest any longer and was about to accost his companion again when Mr. Fox roused from his meditative state.

"How negligent of me to accept that washerwoman's supposition that the man was elderly just because he had poor posture..." Fox said quietly, chastising himself. His countenance changed quickly however and he turned to answer his partner's query. Flashing his wry grin he said, "No, Captain. This time we struck pay dirt."

Shelby's jaw dropped. "He was our man? But how do you know? You did not even question him!" he blurted. "Why did we let him go?" He quickly jumped from the shock of having found their prey to the inexplicable outcome of their pursuit. The captain stared at his cohort, resolutely awaiting a reply.

Fox was silent, but not in a discourteous or sly way. It was obvious that he was weighing how he should respond. Finally he pulled up on the reins, stopping his horse upon the road. "Captain," he began but then paused, his lips a firm, straight line. "Captain, I believe I have figured the solution to the whole matter."

"What? You have?" Shelby returned. He was overwhelmed with astonishment, not merely at the fact that his partner may have solved the mystery but also that he had done so with what appeared to be virtually no new evidence apart from identifying the peddler as the hunched man who had met with the ill-fated woman. "Well Mr. Fox I cannot wait to hear the explanation. Please enlighten me!" he almost begged.

The stoic Quaker spurred his horse back into a slow walk, and the captain immediately followed suit, keeping his eyes fixated upon the investigator's face.

"I cannot," he said, his features noticeably lacking the familiar half-smile.

"Mr. Fox; I must draw the line at your coy games. If you recall, you brought me along on this adventure. I simply will not

172

allow that I be denied access to its conclusion." His voice bore an icy severity that denoted the depth of his conviction.

"You have me wrong, Captain. I will reveal the true ending of this tale to you. However, although I am almost positive; I must be sure. A man's reputation is at stake and I simply cannot solidify my beliefs into fact quite yet. I feel it criminal to destroy a man's character without confronting him first."

Shelby shook his head as if clearing cobwebs. "What are you saying?"

"When we get back to the Sprouts I will attempt to test my theory. I am fairly certain that I can confirm my ideas, after which I will make all clear to you."

The captain did not readily accept this arrangement, and again protested. His partner however was unmoved. He did not respond verbally but his angular smirk conveyed his stubborn conviction to his decision. The young officer began to comprehend the frustrated antipathy Colonel Williams had expressed about the obstinate, rogue nature of the indomitable Mr. Fox.

They rode westward at a steady gait that was not quite rapid enough for the somewhat disgruntled Patriot. He would have preferred that they push their horses a bit harder but his pensive partner set the pace.

The pair traced their way back along the same road they had taken to Ricketts Glenn and at nightfall once again found themselves within the confines of the inn where they had stayed on their way to find Mr. Burrows. The gnomish, surly proprietor was no more congenial than he had been on their last visit. In fact he did not even appear to recognize them. He did however produce a welcome stew the famished travelers voraciously devoured. And although Mr. Fox kept to his temperate ways and drank nothing stronger than tea, the exasperated captain found a degree of solace in the keeper's grog which contained a compelling mix of beer, rum and nutmeg.

Both travelers had taken their meal at the bar but after the stew had been ingested, Mr. Fox turned to his companion. "Secure us a room for the night, will you, Captain? I'll be over there reading should you need me for anything." With that, he picked up his tea and removed himself to a corner table.

Shelby had made no reply to his partner, nor was one expected. It had been Fox's matter of fact way of stating that he sought some private solitude in order to return to his Greek volume. The captain cast an irritated look after the obdurate Quaker and tipped back his mug, draining the last bit of liquid. He pushed the container forward. "Another," he muttered. "And my friend and I will need a room for tonight."

The beady-eyed proprietor re-filled the mug without comment. "Same rate," he said.

The mildly inebriated captain looked at him confusedly and pushed a coin across the bar.

The barkeep accepted the token but added, "No, for the lodging. Same as before."

"Oh," Shelby nodded. The man apparently did remember them. He dug in to his pocket and paid in advance.

The captain looked across the room to where his spectacled partner sat enjoying his book. At first the visage aggravated him. He had been merely sent as a courier to deliver a message and due to Mr. Fox's whim, he had been dragged into this affair. In the duration he had thrice nearly been killed and lost a friend in the process. Now due to the man's eccentric code of ethics he was not even permitted to know the possible meaning behind the whole business. He had arguably saved the man's life on two occasions. *"Does that not count for something?"* he grumbled at the thought. As he glared at the contented-looking reader however, his mood began to change. His thoughts again turned to an analysis of the peculiar character, wondering what events had produced the strange amalgamation that was Mr. Fox.

174

The inn had but few patrons that night, and these seemed to share the same indifference as the owner of the establishment. They paid little attention to either the uniformed soldier or the studious Quaker, content in their cloistered conversations and robust beef stew.

For the better part of two hours the devotee of the pacifist sect sat quietly immersed in the bloody warfare of the Greeks and Trojans while the Continental officer across the room consumed alcoholic concoctions, trying to piece together a probable answer to the mystery surrounding the infamous murder of Jane McCrea.

Shelby mused, "He said that we would return to Gates' encampment at the Sprouts because he needed to confront the man before destroying his character. Who at the Sprouts could be connected with the McCrea woman's murder? Does that mean that she was spying for us or against us? Could someone with Gates' army be a double agent?" The fog induced by the grog had done little to help the inquisitive captain puzzle out the mystery. His eyes had begun to droop, yet he endeavored to carry on with his mental assault on the case.

"Come now, Captain."

Shelby jumped at the hand upon his shoulder.

"Do you see why it is folly to imbibe?" Fox's smirk went unobserved by the intoxicated young officer. "Your wits are now duller than ditch water. Let us hope that a night's rest will affect a cure." He slung the captain's arm over his shoulders and helped the man toward their room.

"It looks as if he's on the other side," Shelby stated, standing in his stirrups.

As they approached the tip of Shodack Island it became clear that the captain had made an accurate appraisal. The ferry was

175

moored on the opposite bank of the Hudson. The pair crossed the mucky expanse onto the island itself and halted near the sturdy tree to which the ferry cable was moored.

"Fire off one of your pistols, would you please, Captain."

The soldier pulled a gun from his belt and held it aloft. He winced before pulling the trigger. His head still ached from the night before and the blast would be most unwelcome to his throbbing temples. The boom reverberated through the atmosphere. A moment later the figure of the ferryman appeared and threw an acknowledging wave in their direction. He turned and apparently called for his boys as the twin crewmen came jogging to the craft. The family had the boat moving in short order, each haul on the rope bringing it closer and closer to the waiting investigators.

"Greetings, gentlemen!" the ferry proprietor called as they neared the bank.

The men dismounted and allowed the twins to lead their horses aboard. "Any news?" It was Shelby this time asking the ferryman if he had any word.

"Some good, some not so good," he replied, as he secured the gate behind them. "Washington engaged Howe some twenty miles southwest of Philadelphia at a place called Brandywine Creek. He was forced to break off the fight and escape eastward. Howe's Hessians captured most of our artillery."

Shelby scowled. General Alexander's brigade was certainly in that fight and he could not help lamenting that he was not there to do his part. "Are you sure the report is accurate?" he asked the ferryman.

"Yep. A courier came through yesterday, taking the news up to General Gates."

"And what is the good news?" Shelby furthered.

"Well, Gates has moved back to Stillwater. Maybe even further north than that."

Shelby's eyebrows raised in mild surprise. Perhaps General Schuyler, and Gates' other critics, had been mistaken about his aversion toward aggression.

"I hear Arnold is back. And Morgan's with him now too."

"What of St. Leger? Do you know if the force Arnold sent in pursuit bagged him?" the captain asked.

He shook his head. "The way I heared it," he continued his report as he and his sons moved the craft out into the Hudson. "St. Leger and his men were just off in their canoes when our boys reached the shore of Lake Ontario."

Shelby grunted angrily at the missed opportunity of destroying St. Leger's force, but the general's disgraceful flight back to Canada was almost as satisfying.

"They say St. Leger's Indians turned on him as he fled, murderin' and scalpin' the stragglers," the ferryman added as if he were making an attempt to ease the captain's disappointment.

"Daniel Morgan has joined Gates, you say?" the Quaker chimed in.

"Yep, that's the word." Between hauls on the thick rope the boatman glanced at Fox's deerskin boots, wondering if his passenger was associated with the ranger brigade under General Morgan.

The ferry was halfway across the mighty river when Shelby noticed that they appeared to be a hundred yards or so downstream of the small wharf that was their destination, rather than abreast of it as he would have imagined. Almost immediately his creased brow of contemplation relaxed as he figured the situation attributable to the slack required of the rope so that it would fall into river and thus not impede boat traffic. However he soon shook off this explanation as they appeared to be drifting still further down river. Suddenly the three ferrymen began to scurry around the craft.

"The rope's snapped!" yelled one of the teenage boys.

177

"What? Impossible!" Despite this denial by the father, his panicky actions demonstrated that he knew his son to be correct.

The horses whinnied fearfully when the craft began to angle as the rope ran out through the iron hoops on the ferry's gunwale.

The boat was now moving with ever increasing rapidity as the powerful current dragged the vessel downstream. "Steady the horses!" the ferryman ordered his passengers, alarm evident in his voice. "Boys, hold fast on that line!" he yelled as all three family members grabbed desperately at the thick cable humming through the iron rings.

"Ahh!" each exclaimed in turn as the rapidly retreating rope burned their hands to such a degree that they were forced to release their grip.

They were now considerably further downriver. The senior ferryman shook his burning hands and attempted to grab at the line once again, with the object of tying it off, or at least looping it around one of the iron rings but the cord was zipping through so quickly that there was not an inch of slack in the line, rendering this one avenue of salvation impossible.

Suddenly the end of the rope flew through the first ring, then the second. Each of the boat crew leapt in turn at the end of the line; but their attempts came up fruitless as it fell into the water and was quickly left behind. Even though the rope had been severed, it had kept at least a slight anchoring influence upon the vessel but now that it was gone the flow caught the rectangular build of the ferry in its grip and the runaway craft began to spin chaotically in the perilous current.

Shelby's heart began to race as he tried to steady his braying horse. The captain was not easily unnerved, but the feeling of complete helplessness and the panic he saw in the eyes of the boatmen had driven him to a sense of impending doom. This sentiment was multiplied tenfold when he peered over his saddle.

His eyes widened in horror. The spiraling, out of control ferry was headed directly for a large sloop that was barreling upriver.

Chapter 17

The boat swirled mindlessly in the grip of the mighty Hudson. The horses tapped into that mysterious intuition animals seem to possess and neighed loudly, nervously pawing at the deck as they sensed imminent disaster. The sails of the sloop billowed under the power of a strong wind. Its prow was elevated due to its speed, apparently preventing its occupants from observing the renegade ferry careening straight for it.

The crew of the ferry had not noticed their looming destruction, being employed in retrieving a coil of rope from a wooden locker affixed to the deck. Finally Captain Shelby was able to force out a yell that alerted the father and sons, but their reaction was hardly soothing. Seeing the sloop now a mere twenty-five yards away the twins let loose simultaneous blood curdling cries of terror and their father simply froze, his mouth agape.

Shelby never learned whether it was luck or divine intervention, but the spinning ferry missed the bow of the oncoming sloop by mere inches as it twirled downriver. Someone from the sloop let out an alarmed shout of surprise as the errant craft nearly scraped the ship's hull.

With a suddenness that startled the dazed captain, his partner dropped his rifle to the deck, leapt past him and grabbed the end of the rope held by the petrified ferryman. He then dashed across the revolving deck and in one motion vaulted up onto the top rail of the gate and propelled himself through the air toward the side of the passing sloop. Jumping from one boat to another as they passed rapidly in opposite directions would have been treacherous enough, but Mr. Fox's hurdle was much more so given that the ferry was whirling away from the ship as he made his leap.

Even though no more than two seconds had expired during Mr. Fox's daring exploit, the mesmerized captain somehow saw the whole episode unfold in slow motion. He waited with baited breath as his partner flew over the ever-increasing stretch of water that spanned the distance between the two craft. Shelby knew that he would never make it. The distance was far too great for him to hope to reach the sloop's deck. Miraculously however, the acrobatic Quaker's right hand caught hold of a belaying pin seated through a hole in the gunwale.

There he hung, the line that trailed from his left hand paying out quickly as the boats parted. Shelby shook off his trance and ran to the wooden locker, retrieving the remainder of the coil of rope the end of which he quickly made fast on a deck cleat. He looked up in time to see two crewmen of the sloop helping Fox over the side. No sooner had his moccasins made contact with the deck then he had his end of the rope tied off on the belaying pin.

The sloop towed the ferry back to its wharf on the west bank and the trio of ferrymen, having fully recovered their senses, moored the vessel to the pier. Captain Shelby carefully brought the shaken animals off of the boat. He patted them reassuringly, doing his best to calm them as a small dingy from the sloop brought Mr. Fox ashore.

"Here," Shelby said, handing Fox his rifle, as well as the broad-brimmed, black hat that had fallen to the deck of the ferry in his leap. "I believe these are yours."

He accepted the items with his normal, wry grin but did not linger to converse. He immediately hustled over to the thick ferry rope wrapped around the large tree. "Give me a hand with this, will you, Captain?" he asked, as he began hauling on the cable.

181

The powerful current tugged at the stout rope, pulling it parallel to the shoreline. The two pair of strong arms heaved laboriously for the better part of five minutes before the rope's end finally appeared as it cleared the end of the wharf. With a few more tugs, the terminus of the line reached the shore.

The family of ferrymen had by now finished securing and inspecting their vessel and had come over to where Mr. Fox was examining the frayed end with his magnifying lens.

"There will be no charge of course gentlemen," the proprietor said apologetically as he dabbed at his saturated brow with a rag.

"Pay the man, Captain," Fox returned, as he slid the gift from Dr. Franklin back into its case. "It certainly is not his fault." The ferry operator accepted the fare, grateful that the men did not hold him accountable for their brush with death

Once they were on the road to Albany, Shelby asked, "Sabotage?"

Fox nodded. "The rope was cut. It was sawed through with a dull, serrated blade to make it appear as if the strands had snapped."

Shelby exhaled heavily in disgust. It now seemed that the man he had killed by the Mohawk was not their only pursuer.

Mr. Fox seemed to read his partner's mind stating, "There is one consolation, Captain. Whoever cut the line is on the other side of the river. He will not menace us for a while at least."

They followed the river road north, again passing through Albany and then further north still. At the Sprouts they found that Gates had indeed decamped and the pair spent a quiet night in an abandoned hovel along the Mohawk just west of the Sprouts. Luckily a large goose had opted for a swim in the river and Mr. Fox's true aim provided them with a meal much more appealing than the cold rations they still held in their saddle bags.

182

It was not yet noon when they reached Stillwater, but they found this encampment vacant as well excepting a number of locals picking through the remains for whatever useful scraps they might collect.

Shelby approached a pre-teen boy whose face lit up as he pulled a broken bayonet from the remains of a campfire. "Where is the army?" he asked authoritatively.

The boy whirled, surprised at the soldier's appearance. He saluted and although the action was somewhat comical, it was obvious that he regarded the salutation with complete sincerity. Shelby returned the greeting and repeated his question.

"Well sir, they headed up to Bemis Heights, about three miles north of here."

"Thank you, soldier," Shelby said, placating the youth with another salute.

"Quite alright, sir," the boy beamed, accepting the praise as an esteemed compliment.

Shelby looked toward his partner who nodded and led the way out of the abandoned camp, following the path worn by the sizable American army.

"Bemis Heights?" Shelby asked, wondering if Fox was familiar with the place.

Fox grunted approvingly. "It is a good place to make a stand. The 'heights' refer to a wide plateau. From atop the heights one has a commanding view for miles. The road to Albany runs below, pinned between bluffs on the left and the Hudson on the right."

"And with Burgoyne's artillery and baggage train, he would have to use that road to move on Albany."

"Yes."

"Could the British flank the heights through the hills?" Shelby asked, his soldierly mind calculating the situation.

Mr. Fox shrugged. "The bluffs are heavily wooded and have numerous streams. It is possible that they would try but I doubt the enemy would invite such an engagement. The British and Hessians prefer open ground where they can apply field tactics and utilize the orderly formations of their troops," he paused. "Their scouts are perceptive, though. I suspect that if they see the left weakly defended they might make a go of it. If they can get a foothold on the hills to the west they could bring up their artillery and force Gates to retreat from the heights altogether. Either way, it is clear passage on the road Burgoyne wants and Gates' army is in the way of that."

As they approached the new base of operations, it was obvious that the Americans had been industriously employing themselves. The heights were abuzz with activity. General Gates' engineer, the Polish-Lithuanian veteran Colonel Thaddeus Kosciuszko had built an impressive defensive network that reached from the Hudson all the way up the heights. The breastworks and ditches included artillery batteries that could easily pummel any force attempting to make use of the river road.

The pair encountered little difficulty in accessing the heights from the south. New troops were still piling in and the pickets and sentries greeted them with a hearty welcome. The upbeat, buoyant deportment of the Americans was a clear contrast to their attitude not long before. News of Washington's defeat at Brandywine had been disappointing, but it could not suppress the favorable circumstances of the Northern Army. This optimism however was well deserved and hard won. Fortune had favored them at Bennington and Stanwix. General Howe had left New York, refusing to join up with Burgoyne and St. Leger was limping his way back to Canada. "Gentleman Johnny's" army, although still formidable, was isolated and his options were running out.

Shelby grabbed a passing solider by the arm. "Excuse me, Sergeant. We have just arrived. Where is Burgoyne?"

The non-commissioned officer stopped and saluted, although he looked to be in a hurry and thus less than enthused at being delayed. "Four miles north, sir. A place called 'Sword's Farm.'" He saluted and stepped to leave but was detained by Shelby's hand on his shoulder.

"On this side of the river?" the captain queried, wondering how imminent the fight was.

"Yes, sir," he returned before trying to leave again.

"One more question Sergeant. Do you know where I can find Colonel Varick?"

After the impatient soldier had provided them with directions to the colonel, he and Mr. Fox hastened across the heights to the man's tent. Before they reached it, a stout figure with a slightly gimpy leg emerged and strode off in a huff. The scowl the man wore was in direct contrast to the jaunty demeanor of the army as a whole.

"General Arnold does not seem happy," Shelby muttered to his companion.

Mr. Fox's crooked smile was his only reply.

"Colonel Varick?" Shelby called into the tent.

"Captain Shelby? Is that you? Come in!"

Both men slid through the opening to find the deputy commissioner-general of musters employed in much the same task as when they last saw him. He slid his chair away from the ledgers and books that littered his work table and came over to his visitors.

"It is good to see you men," he said cordially as he returned the captain's salute. "General Schuyler and I correspond almost daily. He said that he had met with you. How did he look? Do

185

you believe him to be holding up well?" he asked in concerned loyalty.

"Yes," Shelby replied. "He appeared to be fit. He was preparing for his court-marshal. I suspect that Congress will get an ear full."

Varick laughed approvingly. "Sooner or later they will rue their folly. Now Gates is feuding with General Arnold. He's the best field commander here but Gates is upset because he invited Lieutenant Colonel Livingston onto his staff. Livingston had been an aide to General Schuyler and out of petty spite Gates now holds a grudge against Arnold." Varick smiled, obviously enjoying the acquisition of a new ally to share his animosity toward Gates.

"General Arnold is angry because he thinks Gates does not like him?" Shelby asked confusedly as he could not imagine that one with a hide as tough as Arnold's could be rankled by such a small matter.

"Oh no. It is much more than that. General Gates had given him command of the left wing of the army but he moved three New York militia units from Arnold's command to the right wing under General Glover. General Arnold knew this was in retaliation for his recruitment of Colonel Livingston and could not hold his temper. He and Gates had a very heated argument over the issue," Varick grinned.

Captain Shelby remembered that Mr. Fox had alluded to difficulties he himself had had with the mercurial Arnold in the past and stole furtive glances at his partner during this discourse attempting to discern any reaction. However, the Quaker's stoic nature held firm and Shelby detected no change in his deportment.

"Colonel," Fox interrupted. "Do you still have a tent for our use?"

"What's that?" It took a fraction of a second for Varick to register the change in topic. "Oh yes. I will have some men

186

erect one right now." He went over to the tent flap and gave a few hurried orders to a group of enlisted men. "They will have it up momentarily."

"Thank you, Colonel," Fox said, giving a slight bow and then exiting the tent. This hasty departure took the young captain by surprise. He threw Varick a hurried salute and accompanying thanks and scurried off after his partner.

"Take care of our horses, will you lad?" Fox asked one of the privates who had just finished raising their tent.

"Yes, sir," he replied, taking hold of both sets of reins as the investigators removed their bags and saddles and brought them into the tent.

Mr. Fox placed his goods in a corner and pulled his bedroll from amongst the pile. The tent was devoid of the cots and furniture they had enjoyed during their earlier stay in the camp so Fox unfurled his blanket onto the ground and reclined upon it, rolling his black coat into a pillow and placing it behind his head.

"You are going to nap, I take it?" Shelby asked.

"I plan to read a bit first, but then, yes."

"Might I enquire as to our next move?" he asked, leaning against the tent post.

"Tomorrow I am headed back behind the British lines as planned."

Shelby's brow furrowed. "That was what you had planned before we encountered that peddler. After you accosted that Birch fellow you said that we were headed back to the Sprouts where you were going 'confront' someone before enlightening me to the whole mystery." There was a hint of resentment in his voice as he fought to suppress his frustration.

The man noiselessly laughed. "Yes, I said that we would return to The Sprouts encampment. I planned to leave you there temporarily while I moved on. The man I need to see is behind enemy lines."

Shelby exhaled in irritation. "I had assumed that the subject was in the American encampment."

"He is not."

"So then you are still bent on trying to find this Le Loup? Mr. Fox, I know that you are as tenacious as a terrier but I must ask that you desert this plan. We know that many of the Indians have abandoned Burgoyne. And even if the one alleged to have murdered Miss McCrea has not left, he will be with the army. I do not see any possible way that you could confront him without being murdered yourself or at least taken prisoner. I beseech you to abandon this foolhardy scheme."

The Quaker had not interrupted his partner during his impassioned speech and lay unmoving, calculating his reply. Finally he said, "You are correct that before we found the peddler I was set to go after the Indian. However, my plans changed after I identified Birch as the man who had been meeting with Jane McCrea. If it makes you feel any better Captain, the subject of my manhunt tomorrow is not Le Loup, although I suspect that he is still in the vicinity. Now if you will be so kind, hand me my book."

Fox's tone had a ring of finality to it and Shelby had learned that it was folly to argue with the inflexible man once he had decided upon a course. So the disgruntled captain left the tent hoping to distract his mind by surveying the fortifications of Colonel Kosciuszko.

Chapter 18

Shelby awoke with a start. He looked over to where his partner lay perfectly still. He gazed at the man, presuming that he was still asleep. However on second thought he was unsure if "sleep" was the appropriate word. It seemed what the Quaker-warrior called sleep was more akin to a trance upon which he could snap to absolute alertness at the slightest ill-bidding vibration.

The captain stretched and pulled on his boots. He moved as delicately as possible, hopeful that he would not disturb his companion. Dropping his tricorn hat upon his head, he ducked through the tent-flap and wandered out into the pre-dawn air. It was cold; much colder than it had been. Some distance away he spied the flicker of a campfire. Pulling his coat closed he meandered toward the orange glow. Halfway there the delightful aroma of fresh coffee wafted toward him.

"Mornin', Captain," a grizzled infantryman greeted from the fireside.

"Good morning," Shelby returned, warming his hands over the flames.

"Care for some coffee?" another of the men asked cordially.

Shelby smiled. "That would be wonderful."

"There's a pile of clay cups over yonder," the grizzled man pointed. "I expect you can find one that isn't too dirty."

The captain picked through the lot. It was still too dark to see so far from the fire so he ran his hand on the inside and feeling nothing but the smooth clay surface he believed he had found a suitable container.

"Thank you," Shelby said, as one of the soldiers filled his cup.

"Do you think we'll go at 'em today," one man said to another.

"I don't know..." the other replied. "The way I hear it, Gates likes our chances better if we stay on the defensive and let the lobsterbacks come to us."

The grizzled man laughed. "I know one fella who can't stand waiting for the Redcoats to attack. General Arnold has been pitching fits for the last two days."

Shelby was aware that idle discussions and gossip were common chit-chat in any army encampment but knowing the reputations of both Gates and Arnold, he thought it probable that these men were correct.

A pale, pink light had begun to glow in the east. By the time the captain had finished his coffee, the radiance had spread and the features of the men around the fire could be seen without the aid of its flames. Shelby now discerned that one of the "men" had in fact been a boy no older than twelve. The lad looked over to the eastern sky and pulled a drum from behind him. Bidding the men farewell, he looped the instrument's rope over his neck and walked away beating revelry, signaling the American army that it was time to awaken.

The captain moved over to the rampart at the edge of the heights. He exchanged salutes with a team of artillerymen dutifully engaged in the morning ritual of preparing their cannon. Below, a milky-white cloud hugged the valley. The mist formed an impenetrable veil that obscured the flat plain beneath but Shelby's ears revealed just how close the enemy was as the sound of their own drums echoed through the fog, issuing a ghostly announcement of their proximity.

By the time Shelby returned to their tent his partner had eaten, shaved, and was in the process of changing into the garb of the trapper. The cool air did not seem to affect him as he

190

stood bare-chested, although the vicious scar that ran up Fox's left forearm was purplish in color.

"So you *are* going behind the lines?" Shelby asked incredulously.

Fox chuckled silently. "I told you that I was going to do so." The captain shook his head, aggravated at the obstinate man. He began to open his mouth to reiterate his protests but waved his hand in exasperation toward his partner, foregoing the effort.

Mr. Fox had pulled on his shirt and was just slipping his tomahawk into its home at the small of his back when a commotion outside caught the attention of both men. Fox habitually grabbed his Quaker hat rather than the leather hunter's cap sitting nearby and thrust it upon his bare head before both men dashed outside.

Shelby stepped in front of a passing soldier. "What is the fuss, corporal?" he asked.

"The pickets on the east side of the Hudson just reported that the British are preparing to advance!" he said and raced off without the courtesy of a salute.

"Come," Fox said plainly as he led the way to Varick's tent.

"Colonel," said Mr. Fox as he unceremoniously burst into the tent unannounced. "What is going on?"

Varick did not seem to take any offense at the man's brusque manner, apparently sensing the seriousness in the Quaker's voice. "The British are on the move. It appears that we are in for an assault."

"Yes, we have heard that much. What is Gates' plan?" Fox asked. It struck Shelby that for the first time his companion seemed interested in military strategy and he wondered if this was merely a reaction to the gravity of a confrontation with Burgoyne's army or if it had something to do with their case.

"Plan?" Varick harrumphed. "You have already seen it. The fortifications *are* his plan. He will wait for Burgoyne to come to us. He will try to use our artillery to destroy them on the plain

191

and hope our riflemen can cut them down before they can get close enough to mount a bayonet charge."

"Didn't I just see General Arnold headed for Gates' headquarters?" Fox pressed.

"That you did!" Varick roused. "He believes that allowing Burgoyne to seize the initiative is a mistake. Although Gates feels that the enemy will make a frontal assault down the river road, Arnold is concerned that they might outflank our left through the hills and rein down on us with their cannon."

Shelby had been weighing the information. "Would Burgoyne be that daft to come at us straight up the river road? I doubt that they could get close enough to storm our fortifications. It seems as though General Arnold's concerns are more valid. I think they would attempt to use the bayonet only after softening our defenses with artillery and that could only be accomplished from the clearings on the hills to our west."

Mr. Fox pensively rubbed his chin. "Oh he may come down the river road; and even the plain between the road and the hills, but it will likely be to distract Gates so that he can outflank us on our left. If that is accomplished, that force will then push us toward the river and into the jaws of their other troops."

"That is exactly how General Arnold sees it!" Varick exclaimed. "He is arguing his case with Gates as we speak. Oh why were we saddled with this insufferable bureaucrat?" the colonel lamented dramatically. "General Schuyler would not need Benedict Arnold to convince him of the danger; he would have seen it clearly himself!"

"Come, Captain," Fox said abruptly, ignoring the colonel's dramatics. "Let us go find out what is doing so that we might decide how best to employ ourselves." He laughed quietly, "It seems that you have gotten your wish and I will not be able to journey behind the lines today."

192

The pair left the tent but Colonel Varick was at their heels. "There is Colonel Livingston, Arnold's aide," he said. "Colonel! Colonel Livingston!" he called loudly. The young man heard the cries and hastened over. "Colonel Varick," he acknowledged. "I am somewhat busy at the moment..."

Varick interrupted. "Has Gates listened to reason?"

Colonel Livingston stopped. "General Gates has taken command of the right, near the river. He has Glover, Patterson and Nixon's brigades under him there, along with the bulk of the artillery. The brigades of Generals Learned and Poor, under the command of General Arnold are to hold fast on the left side of the heights..."

Varick groaned audibly.

"What of Daniel Morgan's riflemen?" Fox asked of the old ranger who was also under Benedict Arnold.

"I was coming to that. General Gates has acquiesced to allow Morgan's men and Dearborn's light infantry to probe forward as a reconnaissance-in-force from Arnold's position to ascertain if the enemy will try to outflank our left. He said that he would allow the commitment of more of troops if the advance party became hotly engaged. Now I must get back to General Arnold gentlemen. Good day," he said over his shoulder as he hurried off.

Varick was somewhat mollified by the account, although he, and most certainly Benedict Arnold, would have preferred sending his whole force out en mass without waiting to follow the cautious protocols set forth by his commander.

"We will see you later, Colonel. Thank you for your help," Fox said before quickly turning away and walking off.

Captain Shelby bid farewell to the colonel as well and hurried after his partner. "What is your *new* plan?" Shelby asked with a smirk.

193

Fox chuckled. "How would you like to head out with Major Dearborn's light infantry?"

"That sounds grand," Shelby smiled.

"I think General Morgan's boys will not be adverse to one more long rifle, even if it be wielded by a Quaker."

The men went to their tent and retrieved their weapons. Mr. Fox already had his tomahawk and knife but grabbed up his Pennsylvania rifle, inspecting his flint before tossing his powder horn and cartridge box over his shoulder. The captain likewise looked over the flints of his dragoon pistols and then did the same to the carbine rifle he now carried in honor of his fallen friend. He slung his horn and cartridge container over his right shoulder and his baldrick over his left, giving easy access to his sword, should the combat become close quarters.

They hustled out to the western end of the Bemis Heights where the advance party of three hundred of Morgan's riflemen and Dearborn's light infantry were preparing to embark.

Shelby and Fox found the man in command of the force, a Pennsylvania captain by the name of Van Swearingin. "Captain, we are unattached to any unit and have come to volunteer our services," Fox said to the man. The commander eyed Fox curiously, his black Quaker hat out of place with the rest of his buckskin ensemble.

Before the captain could respond, a man in a green hunting frock stepped forward. "Fox? Is that you?" he asked, leaning on his rifle.

"It is. Andrew Parker? Goodness it has been a long time," he squinted, observing the man's features up close.

"Does Morgan know you're here?" Parker asked.

"I do not know. I doubt it," Mr. Fox furthered.

"Well Captain," Parker said to Van Swearingin. "This man's aim rivals that of Tim Murphy. If he's with us, I feel safer already," he laughed.

"Alright," Van Swearingin said hastily, anxious to get moving. "Our scouts have identified that General Fraiser is pushing out to the west, just as General Arnold had expected. They are headed for the farm of a loyalist, John Freeman, about a mile and a half north of here. We're going to settle in at the tree line and give it to them when they get into the fields of that farm."

Captain Shelby aligned himself with the light infantry unit but he was within sight of his partner whose group of riflemen was just off to his right. Carefully, though with good speed, they picked their way through the old growth of virgin wood. The morning fog had long since burned off, and with it, its coolness. Although the sun had warmed the atmosphere considerably, the shade of the forest canopy produced a merciful effect upon the Americans.

The refuse that carpeted the woodland's floor crackled lightly under the captain's boots, in contrast to the completely inaudible progress made by Fox and Morgan's men just a short distance away. Shelby moved ahead cautiously, unaccustomed to this style of warfare. He was careful to follow the lead of Dearborn's men who had worked in concert with Morgan's riflemen on so many occasions. He snaked quietly between the ancient oaks, maples, and pines that towered throughout the hills and ravines. As they forded a small stream known as Middle Branch, a mourning dove moaned out its somber song from some hidden vantage point.

It was close to one o'clock when the Continentals reached the southern boundary of the cleared land at Freeman's Farm. From the cover of the tree line, they surveyed the farmer's fields and the farmhouse and out-buildings nearer the other end of the clearings. Some of the men crept into the field and stationed themselves in a small log hut. Others hauled themselves up into the trees, perched as snipers. A rail fence proved another favorable point of placement and a good number rested their

195

rifles along either the first or second horizontal, sighting down their barrels in preparation for a sign of the enemy.

Although a fair shot, Shelby's acumen was nowhere in the league of Morgan's men and the shorter barrel of his rifle further hindered accuracy at a distance. For these reasons he placed himself last along the rail fence, closest to the place where they expected the enemy to emerge from the woods. As the captain checked his sighting for the third time, an industrious little wren landed on the end of his barrel. The portly, though diminutive bird danced up and down the steel, merrily flicking its stubby tail. The captain's eyes trained on the happy little visitor and he was smiling amusingly at its antics when a blur of red appeared behind the creature. Off in the distance the British skirmishers had begun to move stealthily from the trees at the opposite end of the field. He gently shook the gun from side to side and the tiny bird fluttered off. Slowly the crimson clad men crept into the field, moving toward Freeman's farmhouse.

The riflemen took careful aim, focusing particularly on the officers, easily identifiable by the silver gorgets they wore at their throats. Suddenly from all quarters the Americans unleashed their fire. Smoke burst forth from the trees, the rail fence, even the small log hut. The effect was devastating. Heaps of British soldiers lay dead or moaning upon the ground. Impetuously, Morgan's men rushed forward across the field, prepared to destroy any who remained standing.

Shelby quickly reloaded and rose to follow the riflemen. "Wait," Fox rushed over and put a restraining hand upon his arm. There are infantry in that tree line," he said earnestly, his keen eyesight picking out the red coats hidden behind the trees at the opposite end of the field. He looked around hurriedly for an officer to warn. "Wait here," he said and disappeared back into the brush.

Unfortunately, despite the renown of Morgan's sharpshooters, they had failed to see what their Quaker comrade

196

had and before they could be warned the British light infantry that trailed the skirmishers had brought up a small cannon and opened up on the riflemen's left flank. The thunderous blast cut many of the men to pieces. Bullets whizzed about the field as the survivors loaded and shot toward the field piece. Suddenly above the din of battle a bizarre high pitched turkey call sounded and the riflemen retreated, melting back into the tree line from whence they had come.

Just then Mr. Fox returned. "What was that?" Shelby asked.

"That was Morgan. It is how he signals commands to his men out here in the bush," the crooked smile flashed across his face. "He's sent a runner back to see if Arnold can convince Gates to send more troops this way."

"I saw Captain Swearingin. He was wounded and carried off by Indians," Shelby stated coldly.

"Ah, this way, Captain!" Fox hissed as he trained his eagle eyes on the left side of the far end of the field. Shelby was unsure if his partner had heard his report about Swearingin. He was obviously distracted by whatever had caught his attention. The captain followed the swift-moving ranger as he snaked through the woods at the field's edge.

"Mr. Fox," he called ahead quietly, "We are leaving our troops behind," he said, slightly alarmed. But the woodsman was focused on some object that escaped the young officer and now that they had appeared to move beyond their own detachment he knew it better to keep pace with the sharpshooter than to be caught alone.

Chapter 19

The Quaker moved with an astounding rapidity that had the younger man struggling to keep up. They threaded through the towering trees, moving well left of the place where the skirmishers had emerged. As they dashed along, Shelby concluded that his partner may have spied a scouting party reconnoitering for a path around their flank and was anxiously endeavoring to cut them off before they could accomplish their goal.

After pushing hard for a solid ten minutes they came to a small clearing in the midst of the dense forest. Mr. Fox circled around so that they would be at the far end of the little glade. As soon as they arrived at this spot, Fox pulled his winded companion low to the ground and put his finger to his lips, signaling for quiet. Within seconds the tawny forms of two Indians cautiously entered the other side of the dell, trailed by a uniformed soldier. Both bare-chested braves wore the traditional war-paint of their race, but Shelby had to stifle a gasp when he saw that the impassive expression of the warrior on the left was crossed with a diagonal lightning bolt.

Both Indians froze when they were no more than a few feet into the clearing. Fox whispered to his partner, "They know we're here, lad. It's nearly impossible to out-Indian and Indian. Come on," he ordered, tapping the captain on the shoulder. Fox stood and walked boldly into the clearing. Shelby hesitated but a moment and then followed.

The five men stood for an icy moment eyeing each other guardedly. Suddenly the uniformed man bolted. In obvious panic, he tore off deeper into the forest.

"Go after Lieutenant Jones. I'll handle these two," Fox commanded.

"Lieutenant Jones?" Shelby echoed in befuddlement.

"Yes Captain, Lieutenant Jones, Miss McCrea's fiancé. Now hurry before he escapes!"

Shelby shook off his amazement and darted off after the fleeing militia officer.

Mr. Fox now stood alone against the pair of Indian warriors. All three men held their rifles loosely at their side, an uneasy standoff as each man apprehensively waited for the initial move to be made. It was the unidentified Indian who reacted first. He suddenly shouldered his rifle and fired in one motion. However the canny Quaker had dropped to one knee just as his opponent had raised his gun and while the ball was flying over Fox's head, he pulled his own trigger, hitting the warrior squarely in the chest. But a split second had elapsed and Le Loup shot as well, and with more deliberate aim, but as soon as Fox had fired he dropped his piece and rolled to one side, all but invisible due to the smoke of the rifle blasts.

Le Loup immediately pulled up his horn and began to pour powder down the rifle barrel but suspended his effort to reload a moment later when he saw the unharmed Quaker step through the dissolving smoke.

"So you are Le Loup," Fox said reaching behind him and withdrawing his tomahawk. "I was hoping to meet up with you," he continued, pulling his large hunting knife from its sheath with his other hand.

The Indian dropped his rifle and smiled fiendishly, seeming to take unadulterated pleasure in the prospect of hand to hand combat. His bronze hand tugged loose the tomahawk that hung at his waist and like the white man he drew his knife as well.

"You call yourself *the wolf*," Fox said in the guttural dialect of the Iroquois. "But you are a dog. Only a lowly dog murders a helpless woman," he furthered, using the allegorical language of

199

the natives. There was true hatred in Fox's voice, a hatred that burned even stronger than his beloved faith and one that he had long tried to suppress.

Le Loup understood the words and felt the loathing behind them. However they failed to agitate the Indian. To an Indian warrior, women and children were fair game in warfare and their scalps just as valid a prize as those of uniformed soldiers. He replied simply in his own tongue, "White men talk too much. Let your tomahawk speak."

The usually stoic Quaker's blood began to boil; less from the taunt than the intrinsic malevolence he felt. An uncharacteristic yell burst forth from the man's lips as he charged at his opponent, tomahawk raised over his head. In contrast to the white warrior, Le Loup kept his cool and as Fox reached him, he rolled backward placing his foot in the white man's abdomen, flipping him over in a complete summersault.

Fox crashed down heavily upon his back, the wind completely vacating his lungs. The Indian bounded to his feet and leapt at the prone figure, stabbing downward with his knife, intent to conclude the fight that instant. Fortunately the Quaker was a seasoned combatant and knew the danger of remaining still, even for a moment. He rolled to one side just in the nick of time, however Le Loup succeeded in slashing a nasty gash in the man's arm as he peeled away.

Remarkably, Fox had kept hold of his weapons and jumped to his feet ready to recommence the combat. The Quaker's rancor had settled and he was less impetuous and more focused than when the fight had begun. The two men moved around in an uneasy, though tight circle anticipating the other's assault.

It was Le Loup who went on the offensive, swinging his tomahawk in a vicious backhand chop. Mr. Fox ducked under this attack, moving past the Indian as he did so, slashing at the back of his knee with his knife as he passed. He felt the tendons sever and turned to see his opponent upon one knee. Despite the severity of his injury, Le Loup was close enough to strike and he swung his hatchet with his right hand. Fox blocked this blow with his own tomahawk and spun backward toward the Indian, burying his knife in Le Loup's chest.

The Indian fell backward. A spine-chilling, gurgling noise came from his throat and then he was silent forevermore. The Quaker sat upon his haunches catching his breath. He mopped at his brow with his deerskin sleeve and as if suddenly aware of his injury, examined the slice through the arm of his frock and peered in at the crimson gash on his tricep. Dismissing the wound, he picked up his rifle and reloaded with a thoughtless, practiced efficiency.

He stepped over the body of the first Indian, and walked to the remains of Le Loup. Placing a foot upon the man's shoulder he gripped the handle of his knife and with some effort pulled the weapon from the bronze chest, wiping the blade on the dead man's leather legging. He moved a few steps and bent down to reclaim his fallen hat. Suddenly he heard a shot in the forest and his mind jumped back to his friend's pursuit of Lieutenant Jones. A second later he was darting off in the direction of the gunshot.

Captain Shelby hurried after the retreating form of the militia officer. He saw the flash of the man's red coat through the foliage and dashed ahead, swerving through the trees. He stumbled over his sword several times and in frustration pulled the baldrick from over his head and dropped it to the forest floor. When he looked up he no longer had sight of his quarry. He stood as still as a statue, listening for any telltale sound. The discordant call of a blue jay echoed through the otherwise silent wood. He tilted his head at a slight sound. "Was that an acorn falling?" he wondered. Then an errant "snap" caught his attention. He took a step toward the noise when suddenly his prey took off again. Jones dashed from behind a tree some twenty yards ahead. The harried lieutenant ran with reckless abandon, crashing through the underbrush.

Shelby immediately shot after the fleeing man. Unencumbered by his saber, he gained ground as he followed the militiaman's erratic path through the trees. After a five minutes chase, Jones had reached the foot of one of the bluffs just to the northwest of Freeman's farm. As the desperate man started up the incline he lost speed and the tenacious captain overtook him. Dropping his rifle Shelby made a flying leap. He tackled his mark, the impact causing Jones's rifle to discharge. The blast echoed off of the hillside as the two men tumbled back down the embankment, each falling head over heels until both crashed upon the hard earth at the foot of the hill.

Pushing himself to a kneeling position, Lieutenant Jones spied one of Shelby's dragoon pistols that had come loose from his belt during their tumble. The frenzied Loyalist militiaman scurried on hands and knees, retrieving the gun just as his dazed pursuer shook the cobwebs from his head. Shelby responded quickly and drew his remaining pistol. The two men stood face to face not fifteen feet apart, under the barrel of each other's weapon.

Both men were panting heavily and although the heart rate of each was heightened from the chase, it was apparent that the pulse of David Jones was elevated to an even greater plateau out of sheer panic. Keeping his gun trained on Shelby he back peddled, but found he had nowhere to go with the hillside behind him.

Still short of breath, Shelby finally panted out, "You're in league with Le Loup?!" The captain was still awestruck at this revelation and posed the phrase as a question but the near hysterical militia officer heard it as a statement.

"I had to do it! I had to do it, don't you understand!" he barked, a crazed look in his eyes. "I had no idea she was a spy." He began to weep as he unraveled. "I loved her!" he bellowed, still pointing the pistol at Shelby. "I thought she was only asking questions about our fortifications and numbers and movements because she was fearful for my welfare..." He trailed off. "Do you know what would have happened to me if the general found out that I had been the source of that information?"

"You could have broken it off with her," Shelby said coldly as the pieces came into place.

"Are you insane? Once the jig was up she would have talked." His eyes darted around wildly. "I would either be considered a traitor and hanged or belittled as the world's biggest dupe, ridiculed to my dying day. She betrayed me! She made a complete fool of me!"

Shelby thought back to Miss McCrea's brother's disapproval of David Jones. "So you had her murdered instead," the captain returned icily, "And tried to kill us before we could learn the truth." Shelby's teeth clenched and his thumb moved toward the hammer of his pistol as he thought about the loss of his friend John Rawlings.

Just then Mr. Fox materialized out of the brush. He stepped up next to his friend, his rifle held out in front of him ready to be shouldered in an instant. The deranged man's eyes darted to the Quaker and his feet began to fidget nervously.

"Throw down the pistol. You are our prisoner," Fox said.

Lieutenant Jones looked crazily at Shelby and then back at the deerskin clad Quaker. Suddenly he cocked the hammer of the dragoon pistol and as the captain followed suit and Fox raised his rifle, Jones put the barrel under his chin and blew his brains out of the top of his head.

Fox put his hand on his friend's shoulder. Shelby opened his mouth to speak when the distant thunder of artillery pieces pierced the air.

Whether the Quaker would have buried and prayed over the fallen will never be known as he quickly turned to his companion. "The fight has re-commenced," Fox stated flatly.

"Grab your weapons. Get his rifle too, we will trace our way back and pick up the Indian's guns and your sword as well."

"I am not sure where I discarded the saber," Shelby said, pulling his pistol from the dead man's hand.

The Quaker laughed in silence. "A blind man could follow the trail you two trampled through the forest. Come," he said and started jogging back through the brush.

Mr. Fox not only found the way back to retrieve the armaments, he skillfully picked his way through the dense forest in a deliberate southerly arch that brought them in behind the ranks of Daniel Morgan's brigade where the quartermaster was only too happy to receive the gifts of the three rifles they had taken from their recent foes. The number of men with Morgan had swelled as General Gates had finally assented to the pleas of Benedict Arnold and allowed some nine hundred troops to leave the Bemis Heights to support Morgan and Dearborn.

The two investigators arrived back at the American lines in time to aid in the sea-saw battle that had reconvened in and around the Freeman farm. While General Gates was content to coordinate the battle from the distance of his headquarters atop the Bemis Heights, the irrepressible Benedict Arnold rode out onto the field. Shelby was amazed at the man's sheer bravery as he galloped in front of the line, flashing his saber and inspiring the men. The intrepid general's proximity to the fight allowed him to make split second decisions, moving troops where there was an immediate need.

Burgoyne's Hessians had been assigned to march up the river road to protect the artillery train but when things heated up at Freeman's farm, a detachment of the Germans were ordered to move west to attack the American's right flank. As night began to fall the arrival of the Hessians forced Arnold to order a withdrawal back to the Bemis Heights. The enemy had been left in command of the field, but Burgoyne's forces suffered the worst of the battle. The British had lost some six hundred men, a great many of whom were officers, while the American casualties numbered fewer than three hundred. More importantly, Burgoyne's losses could not be replaced, where recruits continued to pour into Horatio Gates' army, many due to outrage over the murder of Miss Jane McCrea.

That night Fox and Shelby sat together at a private campfire near their tent upon the heights. The men reclined, utterly exhausted from the long, eventful day.

"How is your arm?"

Fox glanced at his tricep. "A camp surgeon patched me up. I'll be fine."

"So, the man you were going to confront was David Jones," Shelby stated, taking a bite of a hard piece of bread before washing it down with a swig from his canteen.

Mr. Fox chuckled softly. "Indeed. I had come to believe that he ordered the Indians to kill the woman. But as I said, I wanted to put it to him before besmirching his name."

The captain stared into the fire for a moment, contemplating the events. "So General Burgoyne actually did send a group of Indians to bring the McCrea woman and Sara McNeil to his camp..."

Fox picked up the thought. "...But Lieutenant Jones also sent his own Indians, hoping to beat them to the task. The two groups met upon the road and Le Loup convinced Burgoyne's men that they could take the McNeil woman, which satisfied them as she was obviously the main object of Burgoyne sending his Indians out given that she is cousin to his lieutenant, General Fraiser."

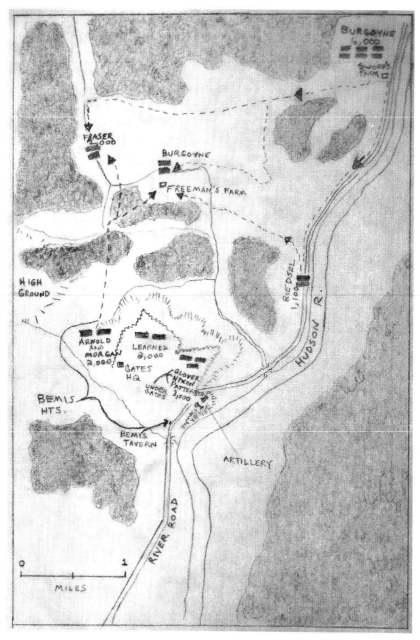

BATTLE OF FREEMAN'S FARM

"And Le Loup told them that he would deliver Miss Mc Crea directly to her fiancé at Fort Ticonderoga, but later claimed that he encountered colonial militia who accidentally shot the girl," Shelby finished.

"That is how I figure it," Fox said through a mouthful of biscuit. What led you to conclude that Jones was the culprit?" he asked curiously. "What was it about that peddler that solidified your opinions?"

Fox exhaled pensively, figuring how much he was at liberty to reveal. "I will tell you, Captain. I said that I would do so, and my word is good. However, you must not put this in your report nor can you speak of it to anyone."

Shelby leaned forward expectantly and his companion continued.

"I recognized that man, Harvey Birch. I had seen him on two prior occasions, both times in the same place. He was meeting with General Washington."

"General Washington?" Shelby gasped disbelievingly.

Mr. Fox nodded, tossing a small twig into the fire. "Few know this about the commander-in-chief, but he is an ingenious spymaster. He has a thorough network. You may have guessed that I have acted for him in such a capacity on more than one occasion." The Quaker sipped from his canteen then chuckled to himself. "I wish that I would have seen the man standing! If so it would have helped identify him as the 'stooped man,' but he was seated both times I saw him with the general."

Shelby interjected, "So when you recognized his face, you realized that Miss McCrea was spying for *us*."

"Not only that," Fox returned, "It dawned on me that Washington sent me up here not only to ascertain the truth about the girl's death for the alleged propaganda purposes, but also to determine if her role had been compromised."

"To see if the group she was associated with had been found out?"

"Exactly. Fortunately, we learned that David Jones told no one as he did not want anyone to learn of Miss McCrea's activities."

"Did he not tell the Indian, Le Loup?"

Fox exhaled disgustedly. "He need not explain himself to such a savage. That Indian would have been ecstatic to be given permission to murder for such a scalp as adorned that woman's head. No, he did not reveal his motives to *The Wolf.*"

Shelby stared into the flames once more. "Do you think her brother knew what she was up to?"

"The militia colonel? It is possible. I doubt we will ever know." Fox drew a deep breath of the cool night air before musing further about Harvey Birch, "His guise as a peddler is perfect, you know. He can inconspicuously move about the neutral ground as well as in and out of the camps of both sides..."

"Whom do you suspect cut the ferry cable?" the captain interrupted the thought.

"Oh, one of the Indians perhaps, or another petty hireling. Someone that would have accepted Jones's orders and possibly money without requiring an explanation."

Shelby thought back to their earliest encounters with the marauders on the road up to Stillwater. "How do you suppose Jones found out what we were doing?" he asked.

"We made no secret of the fact that we had come to make a report about the McCrea girl's death. I suppose he worried that we would stumble upon the truth."

"And he is from New Jersey," Shelby pondered. "He could have kinsmen or friends who found out about our mission from its earliest stages."

"It is certainly possible. If anyone at the Middlebrook encampment, or even in that tavern where we first met had

208

overhead our assignment, and was an acquaintance of Jones, or related it to one of his friends, it would be quite innocent of them to write to the lieutenant offering condolences at the loss of his betrothed and consoling him by stating that an investigation was being mounted."

It is lucky that you spied Jones and his Indians at Freeman's farm," Shelby stated. "As you know, I was less than enthused about you slipping behind the British lines again."

"Luck? Perhaps divine intervention," Fox quipped as his shoulders rocked in noiseless laughter. "Actually it makes perfect sense. We were at the end of our line and a local officer like Jones, especially one accompanied by Indian scouts, would be the natural choice for the British to send to reconnoiter beyond our left to see if our line could be flanked. Once I saw them heading out, I knew that we could cut them off."

The men were silent for a long duration before Shelby broke the quiet. "So what now?"

"Men are swelling this camp as we speak. I do not think we are really needed here. I assume that you would rather be back with your own unit helping in the fight against Howe?"

"That I would," the captain returned, sitting up a bit in anticipation.

"Well then Captain, I release you from your duty here. Tomorrow you may begin your trek back to General Alexander's command at Washington's headquarters. Make out your report stating that Jane Mc Crea was murdered by Indians allied with the British for the sole purpose of her scalp. That will assuage Congress's trepidation about using the girl's death for propaganda purposes. I will provide you with an encoded message for General Washington alerting him of the specifics, including that his espionage network in this area remains uncompromised."

The young officer was elated at the news; anxious to return to his comrades. "And what of you?" he asked as a feeling of melancholy suddenly drifted over him.

"I have some business to attend to near Manhattan," he said as he noiselessly chuckled. "But Captain," his voice turned serious. "I must thank you for all of your help. You were truly invaluable in this endeavor and it could not have succeeded without you. In fact, it is likely that I would not still be upon this earth had you not come along."

He was touched by the sincerity of the usually reserved man. "You are quite welcome," he smiled. "I owe you just as much thanks."

"I think that I shall sleep out here this evening," Mr. Fox said, abruptly pulling his hat over his eyes and reclining fully upon the ground. "Good night, Captain."

Shelby still had not grown used to the man's quirky nature, but he smiled approvingly as he gazed across the fire at the form of the eccentric Quaker-warrior, wondering if he would ever discover the series of events that had created such a unique contradiction of a man.

The captain did not share his friend's desire to sleep beneath the stars and instead lay down inside their tent. He awoke early to the same cool, damp atmosphere that had descended upon the hills of New York the previous morning. He rubbed his eyes in the pale morning light. Somehow he felt that something was different. Suddenly it dawned on him. Mr. Fox's possessions were gone. He stepped outside as the drums began to beat revelry and as the sun crept over the horizon he recognized the face of the young soldier they had entrusted with their horses upon their arrival atop the Bemis Heights.

"Did you see my friend?" he asked.

"The man with the Quaker hat? He rode out before sun up."

Shelby exhaled ruefully, harboring a slight feeling of emptiness as he stepped back into the tent to dress for his own departure. As he reached for his shirt, atop his things he found a small leather book. He picked up the Greek volume. Inserted between the pages was a sealed paper; obviously the encrypted message for their commander-in-chief. He smiled to himself as he leafed through the foreign text. Upon the first sheaf an inscription read:

> To my friend William,
> I pray that our cause to attain liberty will be as successful as the Greeks' efforts to rescue Helen. I also hope that I might call on you again for aid should I require assistance with another assignment.
> Yours in Christ,
>
> Ezra

Epilogue

Burgoyne debated whether to renew his attack upon the American position but decided to delay when he received a letter from General Henry Clinton who commanded the garrison Howe had left to occupy New York City. The letter stated that Clinton was planning to attack Fort Montgomery on the Hudson just north of Manhattan. Clinton did take the fort but Burgoyne misinterpreted his colleague's intentions, believing that he might move further up the Hudson and threaten Gates' army from the rear. This most certainly would have benefitted the beleaguered general who was short on both men and supplies. However, Clinton's force was far too small for such an ambitious enterprise and he had no intent in pushing that far up the Hudson.

Two and half weeks had passed since the Battle of Freeman's Farm and it finally became apparent to Burgoyne that Clinton was not coming to his rescue. He must either attempt an arduous and lengthy retreat back to Canada or risk all in an attack. Despite the objection of some of his commanders and the fact that the Americans now outnumbered him nearly two to one, the natural gambler opted to attack.

During this time the discord between Benedict Arnold and Horatio Gates erupted. Despite the testimony of the field commanders and men who fought at Freeman's farm, Gates gave no credit to Arnold in his official reports. This was something the vain and mercurial Arnold could not let go and he verbally accosted his commander over the issue. Gates removed Arnold from command, confining him to his tent as the Battle of Bemis Heights began. However, the fiery general refused to accept a position on the sideline and disobeyed his commander, riding out onto the field even though he technically was without a command. He bravely and brilliantly led the assault, routing the British and their Hessian allies. Unfortunately a musket ball shattered the same leg the valiant though obstinate general had wounded in Quebec. But the battle was over. The British fell back, losing six hundred men to the Americans one hundred and fifty.

The twin battles of Freeman's Farm and Bemis Heights, commonly known as the Battle of Saratoga, resulted in Burgoyne's surrender. Now outnumbered three to one with no hope of reinforcement or resupply, the British commander capitulated. This proved to be the turning point in the war as news of the victory would eventually convinced France to enter the conflict on America's side.

Burgoyne's inactivity as he waited in vain for Clinton's support had cost him, and the British war effort, dearly. Incidentally, it is rumored that a mysterious individual somehow tampered with the correspondence between the two generals leading to Burgoyne's confusion about Clinton's intentions.

General William Alexander
(Lord Stirling)

Philip Schuyler
(by John Trumbull)

Horation Gates
(by Gilbert Stuart)

John Burgoyne
(by Joshua Reynolds)

Benedict Arnold

Herkimer at the Battle of Oriskany
(by Frederick Coffay Yohn)
Although mortally wounded, General <u>Nicholas Herkimer</u> continued to lead the <u>Tryon County Militia</u> at the <u>Battle of Oriskany</u> on August 6, 1777.

Surrender of General Burgoyne by John Trumbull

Made in the USA
Middletown, DE
04 January 2018